The Roar Went On. . . .

Somehow, Ryoko felt quite free from fear. Even while a hail of death crashed about them. She moved closer to Josh, conscious of some vague, preconscious emotion—

"Didi," Josh said quietly.

Without a sound, the boy slipped quickly aside, remaining part of them but outside, and the two of them collapsed into a shattering embrace.

The intimacy of it disturbed her profoundly. This is all wrong! she thought. Nothing has been arranged, we haven't been introduced by our parents, it's all improper. Her body shuddered with pleasure and guilt, and with the sensuous warmth.

For a few seconds they were three-in-one—somehow the boy was never out of the picture.

This doesn't feel as wrong as it should, she thought. But why?

Then she remembered why. It was the end of the world. And the roar of death went on. . . .

STARSHIP & HAIKU

SOMTOW SUCHARITKUL

A TIMESCAPE BOOK
PUBLISHED BY POCKET BOOKS NEW YORK

This novel is a work of fiction. Names, characters, places and incidents are either the product of the author's imagination or are used fictitiously, and any resemblance to actual persons, living or dead, events or locales is entirely coincidental.

Another *Original* publication of TIMESCAPE BOOKS

A Timescape Book published by
POCKET BOOKS, a Simon & Schuster division of
GULF & WESTERN CORPORATION
1230 Avenue of the Americas, New York, N.Y. 10020

ISBN: 0-671-83601-3

First Timescape Books printing September, 1981

10 9 8 7 6 5 4 3 2 1

Printed in the U.S.A.

for Princess Chumbhot,
sweetest of patronesses; for
Deborah, in memory of Mozart duets; for
Mark, a kid with a kite; and
especially for
Thaithow and Sompong, with love

Contents

Gaikotsu no
ue wo yosote
hanami kana

(Look! Skeletons,
in their best holiday clothes,
viewing flowers.)

—Onitsura (1661–1738)

Prologue

SPRING, 1997

Spring, season of suicides, came suddenly for Akiro Ishida, after a winter of rubber-stamping in his privy-sized prison of an office in the ministry. There had been a phone call, a few hurried arrangements and now this re-union—a handful of young men and a very old one, puffing up the steps of a golden pagoda that overlooked the memory of a great lake.

Nothing seemed quite real here, somehow. The old Abbot smiled, glowed with life, seventy-seven years of it. He was treading the worn steps of the curving staircase easily, methodically, enjoying the squeak-rhythms of the old wood. The Pagoda was tall, for it had been rebuilt four times; now nothing remained of the twelfth-century structure, and the pagoda, in its self-conscious, loving mimicry of the past, seemed to mock what Japan had become. In a while they reached the level where they had overtaken the tops of the cherry trees, and they could see the ghost of the lake, a shallow pool of shadow speckled with puddles, mirror-still in the sunlight.

At that moment Ishida felt Takahashi's breath on his back. He turned around, remembering the man vaguely as a classmate with no friends, another face at the University. Sometimes they had drunk tea with the Abbot together. As they paused on the steps, the two men studied each other with apparent dispassion, but with a gnawing dislike. When they resumed their ascent, Ishida felt faintly uneasy, as though he were swimming in shark-rich waters.

And suddenly they had emerged at the top, where a veranda opened out over the empty lake. Incongruously, someone had stuck a diving board over the edge. . . .

"Beauty," said the Abbot, "and absurdity." He motioned for them to sit down; to Ishida's surprise there was no tea-table on the *tatami,* no utensils for the *cha-no-yu* ceremony. Had he misunderstood, then? Was this not to be a simple drinking of tea, a remembrance of old times?

"I see," the Abbot said, "what you are all thinking. You are humoring an old man, who, when not being profoundly mystical, is often eccentric, wayward, prone to ridiculous gestures. You have all taken a precious day off from your chores at Government House, in your offices . . . and you know that I'm going to come up with some fanciful, perhaps meaningful, revelation. There you sit, four or five young men, squatting uncomfortably on the *tatami,* politely giving me my say." Ishida could see the lights dancing in his eyes, the way the sunlight danced over the puddles in the dead lake. "Ishida—I have invited you here because you are always the doubter. I do not know whether you are angel or demon, reincarnated in this present cycle of being. And, as for you, Takahashi—" Ishida became aware of his former classmate again, felt another twinge of discomfort—"because you are the dark one always, always utterly self-involved."

What kind of game was this? Ishida looked out over the landscape, where the hills, freckle-pink with cherry blossoms, had been skillfully sculpted to hide Kyoto's subsumement into urban Osaka. *There should be peace here,* Ishida thought. *And yet—*

The Abbot sat on the diving board, quite relaxed; the incongruity of it unnerved Ishida still more. Then he said, "Let's have a little doom and gloom, friends, my former pupils. I'm going to die soon anyway—sooner than you think—" The Abbot shrugged off their perfunctory choral condolences, "—and I have a right to sit around and prophesy. . . . You see, Japan has never been so prosperous. Everyone is brewing war, I mean the Millennial War that everyone talks about in such reverential whispers . . . but we are unmoved, almost as if we did not belong to the human race. This does not surprise me, since it is a well-known tenet of my philosophy, that night begins at the brightest point of the day.

"Does three prophecies sound about right?" The Abbot chuckled a little over some private joke not meant for his audience. Ishida was used to this and remained silent.

"Very well then. First, I prophesy that there will be an ending soon, an ending for which some of us have worked and of which many of us have lived in utter terror." He seemed to be looking straight at Takahashi when he said this, and Ishida saw Takahashi start in surprise, like a child caught in the middle of some forbidden act. *He knows us all too well, this unpretentious old man,* Ishida thought, worrying over little secrets.

"Second," the Abbot said, "I prophesy that you, Akiro Ishida, and you, Hideo Takahashi, are destined to cross swords in a desperate battle of conscience, and that this will be your great difference: that you, Takahashi, will wish to die before your death, and you, Ishida, will wish to live before you die.

"And finally—that Man will make contact with a nonhuman species, within fifty years, and that you will both be a part of it, and you will both seek to bend into your own plans that which cannot be bent into human plans."

All this he said quite mildly, without regard for any of its implications. Ishida could not believe him. He was only trying to entertain his students, this old man so near his death; and it was only proper to pay respect to one's teacher. *There is much artifice in the man,* he thought: *his chief delight is in elaborate psychological constructs, and in paradoxes within paradoxes.* But then again he could feel little pity for a man so happy; only envy. For of all those present, in the Abbot's face alone could he see that inalienable serenity, and he longed to taste it and know its secret, but was too secular a man, too much given to doubt.

And then the Abbot was saying, "Take this diving board, for instance—is it not ridiculous, a diving board atop this presumably very sacred edifice? The very incongruity is like a haiku, isn't it?"

Ishida was thinking, *I hope this doesn't turn into a*

haiku-composing party. For he had always been conscious of having an unpoetic mind. He looked at the diving board. Young men had dragged it there some years before, had dived into the lake from the topmost level, daring and taunting each other to ever more reckless feats . . . the Abbot had never complained. He had never cared for appearances; he was too busy contemplating what he had decided was reality. Swimming pools had of course been prohibited for many years, because of the crisis; and then they even drained away some of the lakes; . . . The board's springs were rusty, and flecks of vividly orange paint still clung to the wood, which was cracked in several places. Ishida felt a bittersweet nostalgia for some moments, and selfishly allowed it to wash through his mind like a subtle bowl of tea.

"And what," said the Abbot, "if I were to jump?"

"It's absurd!" Ishida exclaimed—

"It's beautiful," said Takahashi. "To embrace death, still flushed with the joy of living—"

Ignoring Ishida, the Abbot said to Takahashi, "And why is it so beautiful?"

"It is full of truth. It is a poem, a *sumie* painting, full of sadness and regret."

"You were always the glib, skin-deep one!" cried the Abbot in a sudden passion. "Have you learnt nothing from me?" He rose and steadied himself on the board. What new game was this? There was something almost flirtatious about the way the Abbot stood, challenging the sky and the naked lake. Then, more kindly, he said to all of them, "You've all learnt about drinking tea from an empty teabowl. Now I will show you how to swim in an empty lake. . . ."

Suddenly, Ishida realized that the Abbot was going to do it. He could not look.

"Coward!" he heard Takahashi hiss at him. "What kind of man are you, who cannot bear to watch when his own teacher commits suicide with honor, in such a beautiful setting?"

He could have sworn the Abbot was laughing at someone: but he still did not look. And then there was no sound at all—perhaps the sail-billowing of great robes in the wind, perhaps—

Later, they rushed down the steps. They found him dead, and cherry petals blanketing him, soft pink against the white and red.

Absurdity and tragedy—

It would always haunt Ishida, that sunny day of his young manhood blighted by sudden death. But as time passed and a thousand madnesses consumed the world, the Abbot's bizarre suicide would come to feel far less ridiculous, to become even beautiful. For Ishida's mind had been branded forever by the image of that serenity, that peace that always seemed to lie just beyond his grasp.

Part One

THE SOUND OF WATER

Utsukushiki
tako agari keri
kojiki-goya

(Oh how beautiful
the kite, that soars skyward
from the beggar's hut.)

—Issa (1763–1827)

Chapter 1

SPRING, 2022

The million-year silence between man and the whale was first broken on April 3rd, 2022. This did not result from the painstaking teamwork of cryptolinguists and zoologists, for humanity had, for the most part, given up such lines of research as did not meet its immediate, and very pressing, needs; nor was it some lone, half-crazed genius, struggling for decades to communicate with the great aliens who share this planet, who was first to stumble upon one of the most well-concealed secrets of the universe. Instead, this story deals with a young, mildly attractive girl on her first journey aboard, aboard an insignificant fishing vessel (one of the few remaining of its kind) that set sail from Beppu, the City of Seven Hells as the long-dead tourists called it, which is a port in the shadow of the volcano Asoyama, on the startlingly bright green island of Kyushu, a surprising jewel erupting from the poisoned Pacific.

Ryoko was alone on deck when it happened. She was following her father's command, which was always to keep her eyes and ears open: *for there are whole continents outside Japan, my dear.* She had laughed, inwardly, at his solemnity, but had gone to sea an obedient girl.

They were far too respectful of her, though, since she was Minister Ishida's daughter, and so she had been lonely almost all the time. The first weeks she was sick every day, and stayed in the vessel's one minimally sumptuous cabin which they had set aside for her. When she was better, they wanted to show her everything. The boat was powered by sail in the ancient way, and sometimes by electricity. It was, of course, no longer used for fishing. How it worked did not interest her, and she only wanted to see land again and not have to stand on a ground that swayed to a timeless music not of her choosing. So they left her mostly to herself.

Turning from their work, they would sometimes see her pass by, one hand caressing the soggy railings, humming some wailing melody from the classics, for she was quite a scholar; or she would be staring, hypnotized, at some imagined strip of land just beyond the boundaries of her vision.

This time she had been standing for nearly an hour. The boat was hardly moving. She stood stock still, like a statue, her mind lulled by the patterned dancing of light on the water. It was almost evening when the sea crashed open and a great black island stared back at her. She started.

It was a whale.

She could not tell which species, for so far as she knew all of them were virtually extinct. She saw only his hugeness—he was big as the boat at least—and how he thrust the water from him with such terrible force, how he sprang imperious from the swirl with a movement so charged with life that it seemed to fling aside all the hopelessness of the times.

She loved him, then; she was terrified of him, too; and she feared for him, knowing that the oceans were seething with radioactive poisons. And she remembered the sad haiku an old monk had written at the close of the last century, after the Treaty of San Diego:

Oh, oh, the darkness!
The fishes have left the sea
in the midst of spring.

And because she was bereft of words, she began to hum quietly to herself, and because she was lonely, she hoped he could understand her.

But then the whale spoke to her, calling her by name: "Ryoko." It was a liquid murmur that seemed to emanate from the water itself; totally inhuman, rich and elemental. It called out to her as from an unremembered past, and dispelled her terror.

"Ryoko," the water said, and Ryoko was reminded that before the Millennial War there had been scientists who had concluded that the intelligence of whales might be far higher than that of humans . . . but who's to understand what he thinks, then? she thought. It's an alien, there are no common referents in our environments, not even space and time, probably.

"So why are you speaking to me?" she ventured, "and why haven't you communicated with us before?"

He disappeared from sight, and the empty waves whispered: "The first is simple. I am creating sound waves by telekinesis. Our intelligence is not one of hands or tools. To the second question: you do not know what you ask."

He rose again from the depths, shadowy and shapeless in the twilight. Telekinesis, she thought: then why didn't they command the harpoons of the ancient hunters to fall useless into the sea?

"It was irrelevant!" the water thundered.

"On our history tapes, I saw my forefathers killing yours by millions, in the days before the Millennial War."

"Child, O child: you are mayflies that fizzle in the sunlight, cherry blossoms that sparkle as their corpses litter the grass. Your conceptualization of death is so innocent; you do not understand it as I do, and your people's reaction to it is rooted in ignorance and emotional immaturity. No, life is not one of our primary pursuits. A beautiful death is the supreme joy, the supreme achievement of intelligence; life exists only as a necessity for it."

Ryoko's heart leapt with understanding.

"We consecrated ourselves to death many millennia ago, Ryoko. It was a game."

I know about this death, she thought. It is what makes us different from the other races, it's why the whale has come to one of us. My people worship death: the beautiful suicide of young lovers, the noble death of a warrior in the spring. It's the ultimate beauty that pains the heart.

"Child, we must help one another, now."

A breeze came, a sudden chill. There was, almost, no sun. "Help? How?"

"It concerns survival," said the whale. "You humans have not played fairly in the game of life and death.

"We thought we had outgrown our desire for life. We had set our thoughts on eternity, on breaking through the barriers of the material world. But when the survival of *all* came into question—well, even we have not the all-embracing wisdom to accept this. We are, it seems, still bound by our animalness—" he seemed to hesitate. "It is difficult to communicate this to a creature without the concepts. . . .

"Even you will not survive, and most of the animals are already dead."

"No, no," said Ryoko. "My father says some of us will survive." But she thought: *survival is relative.*

And the whale—again he seemed to have read her thoughts—said: "Yes, and we shall all survive, if you do as I say."

"You ask us to help you: we, your killers."

"Yes, yes, and you shall know why, when the time comes, later."

The whale paused. In the darkness she heard water churning, and she wrapped her arms around herself to ward off the cold. She sensed the compassion in him, and loved him still more.

"But what must I do?"

"Tell your father that he and his Cabinet must come to the harbor at Yokohama in six months' time. We will meet there, to discuss what they are building."

"Building? What could my father be building? And don't you have the power to control matter? If you need something built can't you build it yourselves, even without tools?"

And she knew the answer even before it came.

"We are not builders," said the whale, "but dreamers." And he dove into the dark water and was gone.

For a long while she stared after him, shivering a little.

"Miss Ishida?" came a voice, startling her. She whirled around. It was only the captain, telling her she would be ill if she remained. At first she did not answer him, and because he was sorry for her he stood beside her and showed her the stars, giving them fanciful names out of old myths. She looked up politely, not wishing to offend, and pretended to be impressed with his knowledge, but she knew, also, that some of the stars were artifacts from the past, still directing their lethal radiation at long-perished targets.

Afterwards, they went inside, and she found herself surprisingly friendly disposed towards the crew, and they sat talking of little things; but she mentioned the important thing to no one, even though it was still a month's journey to Hawaii.

To ease the loneliness, she would sit talking with Captain Shimada. He told her about Hawaii—about the charred skyscrapers, black skeletons of hubris blood-stained by the setting sun; about the fused sheet of glass, many kilometers long, that would dazzle your eyes and bring the tears to them; about the halls where the young mutants lived, and the hospitals where they lay dying. Not beautiful deaths, they all agreed. He told her about the giant crater inside Halemaumau, the one not put there by nature, and the cliffs that had been ripped asunder.

And all she would say was, "Now I understand why Father has sent me on this journey." And she would wait for the whale to come back, to answer the hundred questions she had for him, now that she could not reach him. Sometimes, at night, alone on the deck, she would fancy she heard the high whinings, the reverberant hummings, the throbbing deep tones that were the whale's song; sounds ancient and compelling, like the music of the old *Noh* plays. But usually she heard nothing; not even gulls, crying over the waters.

At last she decided that she would be returning to her father no longer a girl.

SPRING, 2001

Feebly, Josh Nakamura tried to pry an opening in the sea of legs that towered over him and engulfed him. Everybody in town had rushed to the eruption, had crammed onto the observation decks. There wasn't much for a ten-year-old boy to see but legs and the choking, oppressive wisps of sulphur smoke. He pressed harder, against a tall woman's rump.

"Let go!" He was brushed aside, pulled along involuntarily by the surge, and then he heard the crowd sigh softly, in a single, elemental voice, and still he hadn't seen a thing. Josh couldn't turn back now; he was wedged in, on the edge of the crater Halemaumau, trapped and crushed and breathing poison, suffocating. . . .

And suddenly he was jerked through to an opening between a big black man's legs, and his breath was taken away completely by the splendor of the volcano beneath, he let himself be blinded by incandescent cascadings of liquid flame. Tears sprang to his eyes, what with the pressure of thousands of sweating, panting people and the sweltering heat and the choking fumes and the fiery whirlpool that churned and leapt in burning prominences into the black night.

After the awestruck silence, they whispered among themselves; and little fragments of meaning pelted his consciousness as he forced his eyes to stare unblinking at the volcano's heart: *first eruption here in twenty years . . . and to think, we just decided to come to Hilo at the last minute! Why, I'd . . . D'ye think the enemy did this? Wouldn't put it past them* . . . Must try to stand the pain, Josh thought to himself. And he imagined the fire branding his mind.

And someone was singing softly in Hawaiian, which had died out, officially, only a decade ago. He turned, craning his neck and almost crushing himself against the crowd, and it was an old man with closed eyes. Suddenly uninterested, he strained awkwardly to shift his head so he could take another look at the volcano.

Then came the screaming.

And in seconds, the stampede.

Quick, quick, the shelters!

Walls of screaming, shrill and inhuman, closed in on him and he was pushed along, down the narrow steps of the mountain side. He shut his eyes and clenched his fists and just let himself be dragged by the tide, half tumbling, half pushed, gasping for breath.

A hand seized him roughly. "Do you want to get killed, child?" a voice wheezed in Japanese; then: "Oh my God, it's Josh. *Hayaku, hayaku,* you want to be killed?"

He opened his eyes. Everything blurred, the screaming and the hissing of the mountain and the roaring of the flames. It was *obasan.*

"Grandmother . . ." weakly.

The old woman grabbed him by his T-shirt and pulled

him close to her, muttering "my God, my God," to herself in English.

"Mommy?" he said.

"I don't know where they are," said Grandmother. "Be quiet, be quiet, into the truck, into the truck . . ."

"Grandmother, what is it, what is happening?"

Then he remembered his mother, heavy with child, being taken away in the morning, and the hypocritical conspiracy in the family to hide the things they thought he was too young to know about, and how they had sent him with *obasan* to see the eruption. He did not know what could have happened to them now. But he felt no fear, only a strange dissociation from the terrors that assaulted him.

People were throwing themselves onto huge MacDonalds trucks parked on both sides of the highway. Josh and his grandmother squeezed themselves through a pile of wriggling sprawled bodies, up the two steps. From all the way up the mountain came the thunder of stampeding feet.

"Is it going to erupt bad, grandmother? Are they evacuating us?"

"Will you be quiet, child!" She turned away and began to sob hysterically as she pushed him onto the truck. Her sobs were dry-sounding, like the scrunching of scrap paper. People were pressed sardine-thick inside, clinging to each other, crying softly, trying to breathe. Josh wrenched himself around and looked straight up at the sky.

The moon was in two pieces. So he knew it was the war. But he wasn't scared, yet.

"Don't look at it, just get in . . ."

The doors clanged, the truck squealed and squashed them together like hamburgers, squelching their sobs. Josh couldn't see at all. Flesh pressed against him on both sides. He felt for his grandmother's hand but could not find it. Then the truck took a curve and he couldn't move at all. The whispers began, frightening whispers about death and strange weapons and wars . . . *Honolulu's flat now . . . nobody gives a damn about Hawaii anyway, we're just a damn pawn . . . who's neutral in this war? Japan, maybe?* . . . but Josh wasn't scared, just empty.

Another squeal and they were suddenly still. Silence fell briefly, before the doors grated open and they saw they were about to be disgorged into the mouth of a tremendously deep pit. Uniformed men with truncheons started to push people down towards the hole, where Josh could see the shadowy outline of stairs . . . he started to follow them, still reaching for his grandmother's hand, when, as he reached the pit-mouth, he turned for a last look at the sky.

The sky was glowing softly, with delicate streaks of mauve and turquoise light shifting gently like a fishnet to catch the stars. There were meteors, with bright tails, criss-crossing the luminous night, playing tic-tac-toe against the grid of pastel light-beams . . . broken, the moon floated. Nothing could be so beautiful, Josh thought, not knowing whether or not they were signs of instruments of death. And on the horizon were lines of fires that might have been distant cities.

They were herded down an endless succession of musty, narrow steps smelling of antiseptic and piss, the adults all hunched and bent in the narrow passageway, until finally it broadened and they stood on a moving walkway that still sloped downwards, towards a point of light.

There was no end to the room at the bottom. The crowd did not begin to fill it, and the blazing of massed arc lamps made them feel curiously small . . . Josh stayed beside his grandmother for a moment, listening to the repetitive announcements in English, Japanese, Mandarin and Hawaiian:

". . . survivor control, survivor control. Please give your name, citizen number or alien registration number to Central Computer at once. Terminals are located every one hundred meters in each direction. Do not push or hurry. Do not panic. The situation is temporary."

Josh and his grandmother made their way to a terminal which blinked and flashed a few feet away. He put his hand on the ID plate and said: "Nakamura, Josh: 13249776."

"Re-identify, please. No such name exists on our records."

Josh smiled sheepishly, and self-consciously gave them his real, Japanese name: "Nakamura, Yoshiro: 13249-776."

"Proceed." Josh wondered what he was supposed to proceed to. *Obasan* repeated the procedure. She was shaking now, but Josh was beginning to see things as a great adventure. Here at least there was light, and then, as if in response to his boyish excitement, band music began to blare from unseen sources. Of course, he did not doubt but that the Americans would win.

There was a commotion at the foot of the tunnel. Josh turned casually towards it, and then thrust himself through the crowd as he heard a familiar voice, screaming in agony. His mother had fallen on the concrete and was flailing the air wildly, while two attendants in white coats held on.

"Mother!" he yelled, and staggered towards her.

"Get the kid out of here . . . wait, are you a relative?"

The boy nodded, dully.

. . . poor thing, they dragged her from the hospital bed while she was in labor, they made her get into one of the trucks . . . what about all the terminal patients, all the ones who couldn't walk? . . . they just left them all, they must be pulverized by now. . . .

The people became a wall that screened him from his mother. He heard no more screams. But he looked up at the walls, and then whimpered "Where's my father?" repeatedly at people who dared not look into his eyes. But instead of answering him they handed him a baby to hold, and when he felt the trembling thing tightly against his small chest, he was afraid at last.

SPRING, 2005

Didi Nakamura was five years old when the rescuers came. In all that time he had never spoken, not to his brother or his grandmother, not to anybody. There was too much terror in their world; terror had gripped him since he came tumbling out into it. He could, when he wanted, tune in on their world, but every time he would recoil from it, smarting. But there were other voices you could listen to; soft voices singing to him from a great distance, voices of ineffable beings whose minds he felt he could almost touch.

But even there, he stood on a shadowy perimeter, not belonging.

That first day, Didi ran away from Josh and *obasan.* The Hilton they had moved into had been built during the utilitarian craze; everything about it had been small and soulless. So Didi ran down to the great plain of glass that stretched from the Hilton door to the sea. The smooth glass was hot to his toes and warmed him all over, and the sunlight glared almost unbearably in his eyes; so he had to run quickly, his feet just skimming the surface before he winced with the heat.

He had seen the sea briefly, getting into the truck that had brought them to the new home they shared with three thousand others. When he had seen the sea, it suddenly seemed more home to him than the crumpled skyscrapers of Hilo. For it was like the world below ground; it stretched limitlessly, with no sense of ending. There were no trees, though, and it puzzled him, since they had told him trees were to be expected. There was just the glass plain, sand fused by the unthinkable hellfire of the dead war, glass that ran like a glacier into the liquid glass of ocean.

Didi smiled, though; and the ocean sang softly in his mind.

But Josh shook him rudely. Slowly he came to, grinning a trifle stupidly at his big brother.

"Come on home, Didi. I wish you could talk."

They reproached each other wordlessly—the one for breaking his peace, the other for shattering his vision. *I could have talked to you,* Didi thought. But silence was a force shield, the ultimate defense. It hurt him, though, when his brother talked to him like this. But he would have to stand it.

"Didi, you know something? I asked the rescuers if we'd won the war, and you know what he said? He said, 'I don't know.' "

But that's just it! That's why I don't belong to you, why I prefer my voices! Josh was a tall, handsome boy, but Didi found him too uncomplicated. He idolized him, though; but it was irrational, since Didi was by far the more intelligent. Intelligence was one aspect of his abnormality. Again he wanted to cry out to his brother, but could not, knowing the pact between him and the voices.

"We found an old refridge unit—with frozen food! It's a miracle, how the power stayed on for five years! You're such a lucky kid, you're going to taste a hamburger for the first time . . ."

They started back.

"Oh, come on, Didi. If only you weren't retarded."

Didi took one last wistful look at the sea. At last he knew the source of his voices, at last he knew from what sort of creature they had come, and he knew himself to be unique, a one in a million mutation, a freak. . . .

I have to keep the terrible secret to myself! he thought. *Living every moment for the secret, dying for the secret.*

For a moment he wanted to rush to his brother, to unburden himself, to let him know that this magic that waited for him in the ocean could be his also, if he only knew to listen for it. His brother was trapped in that tiny little *himself* of his. But out there, beyond the horizon, was something that could free him. He started to run up to Josh, wanted to tug at his hand, to cry out, *Oh, Josh, can't you hear the dancing?* But something stopped him. Instead he followed his brother meekly, playing the idiot. . . .

Just wait, Josh, he thought. *They will call you too.*

He clutched the awful knowledge to him as he would have clutched his mother, if he had known her, while the surf shattered ceaselessly against the dead shore.

Chapter 2

SPRING, 2022

Josh had been watching his *obasan* die very gradually, over the past few years. It was not plague, which would only have taken a matter of weeks, eating, like acid, into living flesh, but something more complex, and not quite as easy to grasp as a disease: old age, heartbreak, weakness, many things. He did not care. He had never loved *obasan.*

But now she called him to her bedside. He slammed the door of their little room at the Hilo Hilton and saw her there, gaunt and skeletal beneath the yellow sheet.

"Come here," she said, expecting the immediate obedience due to an elder. This was one of her Japanese habits, brought with her from across the ocean, from another time and almost another universe. He hated what she thought and stood for. He hated the very concept of Japan.

"Under the bed, Yoshiro. The box."

Josh moved slowly towards the bed. He was trying, not very successfully, he thought, to conceal his repugnance. He knelt down and groped under the bed where she hid all her possessions from her grandsons. His nostrils caught a pungency of sick air, but he controlled himself.

"Give me." She spoke in Japanese, as always when she forgot herself. He hated the sounds.

Inside the box there was another box. He handed it to her, and then turned away to unlatch the window so he could get some fresher air, and stood looking outside at where the glass beach glared with the blood of reflected sunsets and the broken buildings, mere skeletons, some of them, stretched from the glass to a forlorn vague distance beyond him.

"Didi!" he shouted. But he did not know whether his brother would hear him.

His eye caught the dark blot on the redness that was the whale.

"A whale was beached, grandmother," he said, defying her with his blatant English. *What a strange thing to happen. I remember people talking about whales, but everyone knows they're extinct,* he thought to himself. And then his mind began to wander: *Today they brought in four more stranges to the hostel. One of them was a new kind, not a feeler or a spider or a dumpling or a veggie. It was as if he had a straight-down gut. I had to clean up the shit while the strange died in my arms. He was four years old! How could a thing like that survive that long. . . ?*

Obasan was saying (but he hardly cared to listen to her) "I hated your father, Yoshiro. He stole my little Eichan and made her into an American! How could he forget who he really was, in only a few generations of living in America? Yoshiro, you don't know, you don't understand anything . . ." (She was talking more for her own benefit than his, muttering in the dark just to hear a friend's voice.)

I wish I could afford a silence tablet! Josh was thinking. *Nights, she talks the whole time, gibbering like an old ghost. Why she* is *a ghost, practically, as it is.*

"Didi!" *Damn the child, the child . . . how old is he? twenty?*

"Let me tell you how I came here through the Pashihiku ocean, before the Millennial War . . . let me see, everyone was writing in *kanji,* not the ridiculous roman script . . . I used to watch *terebi* all day, three-dimensional, we had a new set, when I was a girl . . . they had the old, two-dimensional samurai movies too, reruns, I remember, sponsored by Fujicolor and Makudonarudo hamburgers . . . I came here over the water on a superbird, your father dragging me the whole time, I cursed him, I told him he could never steal Eichan from me, I told him he should go commit *seppuku* for desecrating the sacred name of Japan . . . we were standing in the airport, the Narita monorail was on strike . . ."

How many stranges are there on this island anyway? Josh wondered. *And why are they rounding them all up, bringing them to the hostel to die? On Oahu they're killing them on sight. . . .* But Josh remembered that the four thousand a week from his job at the hostel was keeping him alive, if only barely. *I wonder if it's mercy or sadism, on Oahu. Last week, guy told me you could eat them. . . .*

"Pay attention to me, Yoshiro!" his grandmother snapped suddenly. Then relapsed into her droning catalogue of the past. "We came here on a superbird, Yoshi, in just three hours we came to Honolulu!" (*What is a bird?* Josh thought. *Some imaginary creature.*) "Look, look at what's in this box. It's for you, when I die."

Josh became alert for a moment, thinking of something valuable that he might be able to sell.

He walked over to the bedside, the stench of the room assailing his senses as he turned round again. And—

It was just a twisted old teabowl. Her hands curled shakily around it, clutching it like something precious.

". . . it's *temmoku,* Yoshiro, from the tenth century! My grandfather gave it to me . . . take it, take it, I don't have anything left now."

He took it from her hands. It was so ugly; so like a strange, distorted from perfection by age and by an almost infantile, random-looking application of the black glaze. But it felt cool. Alien.

"Use it to get away from here! Sell it, go to Japan . . ."

Josh was sorry for her suddenly. *My brother is a strange, after all,* he thought. *Like this ridiculous old thing.* And, smiling, "Grandmother, don't be silly. How can this old thing get me off this island?" *It must be one of those* Japanese *things, the ones she's always telling me I'm incapable of understanding.*

Just then Didi burst into the room, though.

He ran to the bed. He had a shine to him, Josh thought, as though something wonderful had happened to him. He came and stood by the bed, a strangely ageless creature, a paradox of nature. Automatically Josh came closer to him, away from the window, protective.

Didi had taken the old teabowl in his hands and was staring deep into it as though hypnotized. Was there something he saw in it, something he shared in common with grandmother, one of those *Japanese* things?

A smile touched the boy's lips briefly. Josh almost touched the kid, then turned aside, feeling himself an alien. "Grandmother, shall I not let him play with it?"

"No, no. Let the boy play with it. Look, he appreciates it." (Grandmother always maintained that Didi understood everything she said.) Josh was a little bitter, there was something between those two that made him an outsider, even though his brother was a strange . . .

"I'm going."

"Yoshiro—"

But where would he go? He could wander the corridors of the hotel, back and forth, seeing scrawny scarecrow people gibbering in dark corridors. He remembered the world underground, during the long time of the war when the lights had never been turned off. Now there was no light at all. He could wander through the corridors, in and out of the mugger-haunted shadows, past the stranges turned beggars, past an occasional plague-corpse with its texture of old green pepper pizza and pistachio ice cream (childhood memories, of course—there was none of that in *this* world). There were legends of headhunters, somewhere on the fiftieth floor.

"Grandmother, I'm going out." But his resolve was weakening.

Or he could go on the beach. He could go and see the beached whale people were talking about.

Didi was beside him quickly, still clutching the bowl. They both went out into the twilight of the corridors; Josh still had no idea where he was going.

"Come on, let's go over to a window so we can get some light," Josh muttered. They walked on for about twenty rooms, groping their way some of the time, once stumbling over a body or something. "Hey, quit grinning over that old piece of crockery. You'd think it was valuable or something . . ."

They reached a little window and stood in the little strip of light. Dust-motes danced. Odors were brighter than colors: faint odors of urine, of alcohol, of some of the new drugs, of silence tablets, too.

"Hey, Didi, do you think we'll ever get out of this place? Yeah, I know you don't understand."

They were squeezed into the light ray. The dank dark pushed oppressively.

"We've got to get out of here, Didi!"

His brother touched him. He was soft.

Didi came to the beached whale.

It was cold there. The smooth glass stole the warmth from his light footsteps, and the wind whipped through the holes of his shorts, but he ignored them all, mesmerized by the alien music in his mind.

Why are you calling me?

He stood still. The huge gray mass of dying flesh lay, as if disgorged from the bowels of the gray ocean, higher than he could see over . . . Didi gazed for a long time at him.

There were boys there, one a normal, the other a strange, lopsided, twisted, throwing a fluorescent frisbee, the startling pink thing shooting back and forth against the big darkness.

Why?

(He was a man now, but had kept the shape of a boy. He was a strange, too, of course; but most people didn't notice, because he didn't *look* all weird and misshapen. But long before the night of the broken moon, the gene-changing radiation had touched his mother . . .)

"Didi! Come back, grandmother wants you!"

But he ignored his brother's distant shout. His brother should have been at work anyway. He worked at the hostel for stranges, the ones who couldn't help themselves and had to be nursed until they died. He had never been there, but had seen it in his brother's mind, sometimes; it was a shadowy place even though lights shone blindingly, day and night. The shadows came from Josh's mind, of course. When you saw things through other people's eyes, they were colored oddly sometimes, by their preconceptions, by their fears.

But now no man's thought could penetrate him. He was drowned, flooded, intoxicated, by a far more powerful music.

The setting sun touched the whale from behind.

You are my brother, he thought at him.

He was smiling, so gently, knowing but not quite comprehending the whale's experience of ultimate joy.

("Yes, brother," the whale whispered in his mind. The voice was so close, like the voice of a twin.)

Whoosh! the frisbee sang.

Yaaaay! the strange shouted, without reverence, without tact. Didn't he know better than to mock the dying of a great whale?

It's Didi, the idiot! the other one was yelling, but the words sounded incredibly faint, as though from another dimension. Get away from him, quick, before he turns you into a jellyfish!

Ugly thoughts touched him for a second. He threw them aside, all the sounds and the sights and the smells and the coolness of the glass beach, and his mind crashed open, like a bursting dam, so that he could see indescribable thoughts, like burning crystals in a cosmic haze. And he knew the thoughts to be not the thoughts of humans, but yet somehow his own thoughts. And he was made to know, at last, who he really was.

It made him crazy with happiness. He spun around and around, laughing wildly, forgetting the other children.

"Hey, this dude's crazy . . ."

"C'mon, let's get out here . . ."

The boy spat, and thump-thumped against the glass beach, running towards the Hilo Hilton up there in the mid-distance.

And there he was, alone with the whale.

(The music of the deathdance came, too, ever so distant.)

"Why did you call me?"

("It is my time for Ending, Takeo"—the whale used Didi's real name, and this, in itself, was a wonder, for no one had ever shown him that much respect before—"the process of revealing the truth has already begun. Some of our brothers have talked to a certain woman . . . but look, I must die here, see, behind . . .")

Didi ran around to the other side.

A harpoon was edged deep in the whale's flank, oozing a glacier-like half-hardened stream of blood. The harpoon was broken . . . a jagged fragment lay on the glass.

But who can have been hunting you? Nobody hunts whales, anymore, that's a twentieth-century thing. Isn't it?

He picked up the piece of metal. There was lettering on it—Russian, perhaps? He could not read it.

("Touch me, Takeo." The whale did not mean *touch me with your body,* but rather something more intimate, a melding of perceptions. "I had been on my way to the deathdance, but . . . some great fortune plucked me away. There are still whaling vessels sometimes, it seems, haunting the sea like specters, trying to conjure up the old things. The Russians perhaps, or islanders. . . . But now I feel a need for not-aloneness, for the thoughts of a brother.")

Didi's mind opened wider and wider. *I'm going to collapse!* he thought wildly. But his mind opened still more and more, like a flower touched by dew, until . . . there were flies buzzing over the caked bloodstream. Someone had hacked away a little piece for his supper, too. The whale's thoughts were weakening now. He saw the glass beach mirror and re-mirror thousands of red sunsets, so that the whale seemed to be resting against a cold fire.

Faintly, he heard "Home to grandmother, Didi . . ."

("Go home, now. Your grandmother won't last much longer, you know.")

But he hardly felt any guilt at this. As he turned to leave, he felt an almost unbearable pang of death-longing emanating from the whale. *I'm sorry I'm sorry I'm sorry* his mind whimpered like a struck child's.

Now a small party of kids, all stranges, such as a waddler with no arms, a feeler with no eyes, a spider with extra vestigial arms, came laughing by, bashing stones against the glass, pelting the dark formless vastness . . . nibbles of pain drizzled on his consciousness. But each stab came weaker than the last. ("Go home, child. There's nothing you can do. We've set the stage now. But you must try to save yourself, you know. I'll show you a way to the stars . . .")

And Didi saw clearly, how the whale was struggling, against his yearning for Ending, to make one last image vivid for him, how he was struggling against forces beyond life, out of compassion for a boy who had never spoken. (And almost, a word escaped hs lips. But the fear caged him, now as always before.)

The whale showed him the spaceship, waiting in the black vacuum, above his head somewhere. It was a ghost from before the Millennial War.

It was so tiny! Such a tiny object, all angles, all sharpness and multifaceted brilliance and hard edges, etched bizarrely into the soft night . . . *it's so small! so precarious! can it really last through a voyage of thousands of years?*

("I don't know. Goodbye goodbye goodbye . . .")

Don't go away, please, tell me some more, don't die, oh god don't, one more word. . . .

("My child.")

The silence thundered, the way speech had never done.

It was so hard for him, turning his back on the whale, then walking, step by step, slowly, then jogging, trotting, running, sprinting up the slippery glass beach to the Hilo Hilton, bursting with grief and joy.

Chapter 3

Josh saw the girl from Japan several times in one day. . . .

Once, sweeping the hostel floor outside the room where some of the more spectacular strange ones were. Spiders, with extra limbs; veggies, with nothing at all except the minimal body functions, apes—the ones with hair growing all over them, that had to be trimmed every day. Sometimes people came here to gawk. Once or twice a year—as today—even a tourist from some other place across the ocean. But here a stranger was safe, by an unspoken law of the island; he couldn't be hunted or beaten up, at least not until he died. . . .

The girl from Japan was arguing with someone, rather vehemently, a man who constantly deferred to her; he glimpsed them in there through the open door.

"But it's so monstrously unfair!" she was saying. She seemed on the verge of tears.

"Miss Ishida, that's just the way things are here!"

". . . I'm not surprised that every other person in Japan is contemplating suicide, then . . ."

She came out, followed by an entourage of people, from

a ship, it seemed. They were all speaking Japanese, a curiously formal kind that was quite quaint, not the kind *obasan* spoke or the other Japanese Hawaiians he knew.

She stopped for a moment, and their eyes met. He saw that she looked at him as though he were a part of the hostel's trappings, that she was used to a lot of human trappings. He didn't like her, not the way she looked at him or the evidently false compassion in her face. And then they were gone, their kimonos—so incongruous looking, garish against the harsh gray of the corridors—swishing and fluttering.

He thought nothing of it, and returned to his work.

Twelve stranges died that morning. Sixteen were brought in from a far part of the island. No new types.

Then he was sitting in the canteen with half-a-dozen other scrubbers of floors, drinking a cup of the protein mush that the hostel lab was experimenting with. It was made from recycled strange corpses, the rumor went.

He clanged his cup on the metal table, scratching the gray paint.

"Did you see the tourists?" said Mokupuni.

"Yeah. Tourists. Ha!" said someone else.

"Tourists?" said Josh politely.

"Yeah, from Japan. Real important people. VIP's. One of them, her father runs a Ministry in Tokyo."

"What's a Ministry?" another voice piped up.

"Oh," Mokupuni went on, "sort of like the King of Hawaii and the King of Oahu and the President of California."

"They seem really snotty," Josh volunteered.

But they all came in, suddenly, killing the chatter. Josh saw them, again bright and ridiculously beautiful, straight and healthy and tall, like puppets, like manikins. They made the whole place so embarrassing.

And then the group filed out again. They had been there only a second or two, but the conversation, such as it had been, never picked up at all.

Two more stranges were brought in during the lunch hour, but they were both already dead.

And then again when he was holding a strange in his arms. It was only a little kid. There was nothing wrong with it to look at, it was a beautiful child, an angel. But everything was as wrong as it could be, inside, it was a jumble of misdirected plumbing and misplaced organs and missing tubes and upside-down valves—

Just as it died, the girl walked past again.

She reached out as though to touch the kid, but Josh jerked it angrily away, as though it would be polluted, thinking *what a stupid thing for me to do!*

She was about to speak to him, but. . . .

"Miss Ishida!" said a voice somewhere in the corridor. There was a strange light and Josh realized that someone was shining a flashlight in the dark room. He had seen one when he was a kid. When he looked up the girl was gone, and the child was just as dead.

In the corridor, Mokupuni said, "I'm gonna stow away, you know, on their ship. Plenty of jobs in Japan. Think they'd hire me? I mean, at least I'm not a strange. Well—"

Nobody else volunteered to say anything, so he just droned on: "You know, millions of people going to Japan every year, you know they have no plague there, they have cities, they have electricity, they have McDonalds, even, remember those?"

"Do you think I could go?" Josh said. But he didn't mean it.

"Hell, yes! I mean, you *are* one of them, I mean you're a Jap, aren't you?"

"I'm American," Josh replied testily.

Didi followed Josh down the corridor in the half-light. "Let's go and find the preek," Josh said. There was a preek who lived in their corridor. He didn't have a room to himself, he had no family, so he lived in what used to be an entertainment booth.

There was no door.

"Hey, preek . . ."

"Yes, come in," answered a timorous, high-pitched voice. The preek was just a kid, around fifteen perhaps. Didi followed Josh as they went in, into a harsh light made artificially, one of the few that worked in the Hilton, somehow. The preek claimed *he* made it work.

"You want to know the future, the past, the present?" the preek inquired. Didi saw him now, a thin boy like a twisted ragdoll, all his grubbiness made blatant by the light . . . and looking around he saw old machines, strange alien machines with wondrous flashing lights and tingling ting-ting-tings, some heaped up in piles, others standing apart, almost oracular.

A three-dimensional pageant played itself over and

over again on the surface of a silvery table: boys in archaic clothing, under a bright sky surfing. They looked like beings from another world, in their late twentieth-century skinsuits . . . over and over the scene repeated itself, a loop in time.

"Well, what shall I tell you?" Ting-ting-ting. "I am a class A precog and can tell you anything!"

Josh said: "Anything will do, Joey, we're just here to amuse ourselves. Anyhow, you're not a class A preek, they'd have taken you away to experiment on if you were."

"Ha!" the ragdoll-boy laughed, a cracked laugh like stones shattering on the glass beach. "You want to know about the girl. Shit, you're just crazy about that girl!"

"What do you mean? What girl?"

But Didi had caught an image of her, the haughty Japanese girl who had been in the hostel, who had seemed to feign compassion but could not feel it because she was not part of their world. He felt the preek pluck the image from Josh's mind like a flower.

Since his encounter with the whale he had become ever more aware of his ability to invade the thoughts of others. It wasn't so much telepathy as a sort of eavesdropping that made him feel dirty, sometimes, and also lonely. For no one saw *his* thoughts except the whale. And he was dead.

"Oh," said Josh. "I hated her, though. But I'm intrigued."

"So meet her, talk to her."

"Why should I?"

"Because you already have!" Again the laugh of breaking glass. Didi penetrated the loneliness of the preek, too, how he was forced to live only one part of his experience, in slow linear progression, even though he had already lived it, future and past . . . he was a traveler trapped in time. The room ting-ting-tinged over and over again, the colors flashed merrily, the surfers surfed, the room seemed to kaleidoscope around him.

The preek twitched and teased his hair. Josh swatted a mosquito with his palm . . . "Think there's a chance I'll ever get off this island?"

"Where would you go?" Ting-ting.

"I guess there's only one place *to* go, really . . ."

"Yeah. Japan. And you hate Japan, don't you."

Ting-ting, ting-ting-ting-ting-ting . . .

"I guess so."

"Yoshiro Nakamura—" Didi saw his brother wince at the full, Japanese version of his name—"Nakamura Yoshiro," he said, then, inverting the surname-given name in the proper Japanese fashion, plucking it from his mind, perhaps. "You're thirty years old, close enough. Your occupation is wiping vomit in a hospital where mutants go to die. Ha! It's uncanny, isn't it, the way I know everything . . . well, of course you've been here before, millions of times, even though *you're* thinking, it's the first time you've set eyes on me. I replayed all the scenes of my life over and over, I couldn't even kill myself if I wanted to. But the point is, why on earth would you want to move on now? what with the world coming to an end and all?"

"Joey, can't you just prophesy? I've had an awful day, I just want to be entertained."

"Yeah, sure. Well, yes. You *are* going to get off this island. But I won't spoil the fun by telling you how you're going to do it."

One of the machines began to glow a dull red, then flashes of laser-like light shot out from it, criss-crossing an imaginary night sky. Except there was only one moon.

Didi suddenly saw, through his brother's eyes, or through the eyes of a petrified ten-year-old, the eerie beauty of colored strands fishnetting the sky-veil, graph-papering the gauze of night.

Then with a zing-zing-zing the image dissolved and the ting-ting tinkled and clanged and an op art labyrinth in fluorescent green danced and whirled on the peeling wall. . . . "Sit down, why don't you," said Joey. "Or are you guys too scared?"

They both squatted down on the cement floor; Joey the preek flopped bonelessly down beside them.

"I'm going to make it, huh?" Josh said.

"Hell, you don't believe me anyway. You think I'm just saying what I think you want to hear because you'll be happy and give me a million dollars so I can buy a quart of fake eggs."

"Am I supposed to believe you?"

"Well, you're the one who said I'm not a class A preek."

"Oh, come on. Preeks are unstable anyway, they're liable to lie at the best of times. Had a preek at the hostel last year, scared the shit out of a nurse by telling her she was about to get killed by a falling building. It didn't happen."

"Well, some preeks see into different timelines than this one . . ."

"That's just a play on words."

"Maybe."

"Didi, let's go."

"You'll be back," chuckled the preek.

The pseudolasers gridded the walls again, blue and red lines knifing through clouds . . . "I can't look!" Josh cried out abruptly, turning towards the door. Didi turned with him, a shadow.

Didi shadowed his brother back into the dark.

His brother was thinking: *now what shall I do? I don't want to go back and watch the old woman sliding further into death. I gotta go somewhere!*

Didi saw that—without apparently meaning to—they were heading towards the stairs. They only had ten floors to climb before reaching the elevator that worked.

. . . but the whale had gone.

The two of them stood by themselves in the shattered moonlight, which blackened the ooze of blood-traces on the glass. The beach was spangled with star-reflections. Josh said to his brother: "It's gone, then. I guess it'll turn up in our food or something." He was slightly disturbed at this; why he could not tell, for he had eaten, knowingly, many far more unpleasant things. "Didi . . . when grandmother dies, we'll all go to Oahu maybe, stowaway on a boat somehow. It's a rat-race there, they say, but here it's just dull; nothing but people dying. On Oahu they hunt the stranges, you know . . . hunt them and eat them."

He couldn't bring himself to think of his brother as a strange. "I wonder what the whale was doing, dying here . . ." he went on, talking to himself, really, since he did not believe that Didi could understand anything but the simplest instructions. "Maybe it felt the way we all feel. This island is really for people who have nothing to do but die. Everyone's given up! What kind of entertainment is there, running around mugging people in hotel corridors? I don't belong, Didi, I'm alive."

Didi was crying, very softly.

"What's the matter, kid? Maybe some of the things I say do get through to you, don't they? Hell, maybe *oba-*

san's right about you. Maybe you're just biding your time or something. Maybe you're ten times smarter than all of us. But I doubt it."

In the moonlight, a slender shape moved in the half-distance, no more than a robe puffed out by the breeze. Josh froze suddenly, recognizing the girl from Japan.

"Let's not go back yet," he said.

What was she doing there, away from all her hangers-on, unprotected? Didn't they have wild stranges in Japan, or thieves, or any of those things? She was quite alone. The smoothness of the glass reflection made seamless the horizon, so that she appeared to be floating aloft, in space among the stars.

"Let's go and see, Didi."

Stealthily Josh stepped in her direction. Even nearer, she seemed unutterably distant. She was staring out to sea, as though hypnotized, waiting, poised and tensed as though she were about to dive . . . she had heard the two of them.

She looked up in dismissal—they were within shouting range, and coming closer—and then seemed to change her mind.

"Ah," she said. *"Nihonjin desu, ne?"*

"Amerikajin da yo." Josh tried to conceal his disappointment at her prosaic question, which had been only natural. "I'm *American,*" he repeated, pointedly in English.

"Oh, I am sorry," the girl said in a strange accent. They looked at each other blankly for a moment. "But you look Japanese . . ."

"My name is Josh. Yoshiro Nakamura. I'm second-generation."

"Oh, I am sorry," she repeated. She turned and started to rearrange her dress, which the wind had upset a little.

"I saw you before, in the hostel where I look after the stranges."

"Stranges?"

"You know, mutants."

"Your son?"

"No, it's my brother. He doesn't talk. He's a little bit strange, too, but not enough to be at the hostel."

"I am Ryoko Ishida."

"Yeah, daughter of the King of Japan or something . . ."

"No, we do not have Kings in Japan. In Hawaii?"

"Yes, there are at least three Kings in Hawaii. They all have gangs of wild people and they go around killing people, but usually they don't come near the hotels or the town. They're not showing you any of that, I guess."

"No, I did not know that America had split into different governments."

"Oh, that! Who knows about government and things? We just keep on living, that's all."

She was a peculiar one, Josh decided. How could they have things like governments? Everyone knew that nobody was running the world these days, it just went on and on on its own. "Is there a government in Japan, then? You mean your father actually controls things, or something?"

"Most certainly!"

It was disturbing. "Why did you come to Hilo?"

"My father commanded me. I was to see how the other countries were, the ones that had been destroyed by the Millennial War, so that I would understand better what we have . . ."

"Well, tell me something. What *do* they have there? Is there really that much difference?"

"But of course there is . . . we have no mutants, not much plague, a government, everything still works, after a fashion, we have electricity and cars and even one bullet train a month between Tokyo and Sapporo . . ."

And Josh found himself profoundly tempted.

"But are there many Americans? Could I get there somehow, get, you know, a job, and all that?"

"Our driver is an American," she said. She spoke of other worlds: worlds with drivers and trains and things. He had always hated the very idea of Japan, but perhaps it was his only hope.

"I want to go there, can you help me?"

"I don't know how, Mr. Nakamura," she said. Then she lost interest. She was a cold girl, he felt. She looked away again, to sea, and suddenly Josh noticed that Didi was smiling, really happily, as though he had a new toy, and that he had moved between the two of them and was stroking her arm, wonderingly. She ignored them both, concentrating on something far out there, something in the ocean.

I don't like you, Josh thought. Then he said, almost to himself: "So there's a country where there are no mutants.

Where plague is still rare. It might be a temporary refuge . . ."

"But what is there to flee from, Mr. Nakamura?" the girl spoke up suddenly. She had averted her eyes from the sea with a kind of bitter disappointment, as though she had been expecting to see something rise from the waves, he thought.

"Death," he said.

"Well, there is no way of escaping. Everyone knows the earth is doomed. That we, at any rate, are doomed."

"Yes, but *I* can't accept that!"

"How un-Japanese you are, Mr. Nakamura! If I were you, I would be able to accept my fate quite graciously. Humans have ruined the earth and it is only honorable that they should die, is it not?"

"Everyone always thinks I have to act like a Jap, just because of the color of my skin. You should know better, Miss Ishida."

"Well, it's a very Western trait, I understand, to want to escape the inescapable . . ."

"Well that's it! I want to go on *living, living* till the very last minute that I can still breathe! My *obasan* is always telling me how people in her country love to commit suicide, she's got an infinite number of grisly stories about that kind of thing. Me, I think if I stay on this island I may as well *be* dead."

Didi's smile had broadened to a delightful grin.

"Well, your brother seems happy," the girl said.

"Yeah."

The moons vanished behind a cloud. For a long time neither of them spoke. Only the water spoke. The sound to him was harsh, like the clanging of cage doors. But he saw how she listened, spellbound, almost intoxicated, and he wondered about her, how she seemed so impossibly serene. *She's just like* obasan, *in her way.* But with her he felt no annoyance. He only felt like an intruder.

"Well . . ." Josh began uncomfortably, "I really came to see the whale. I guess I'll go now."

"The whale?"

"Yes, there was a whale beached here. I think they've taken it for the food machines."

"But that is terrible! Don't they know that—"

She turned her back on them both, and buried her head in her arms, and started to sob, uncontrollably, like a child who has lost its mother. Didi was jerked aside, and Josh saw him standing, staring at his own hand . . . the sobbing was small in the vastnesses of starry sea and starry glass and starry night.

"Have I done something wrong?" Josh felt somehow guilty; he tried to put his arm around her shoulder, but she thrust him away with surprising vehemence.

"Couldn't you have buried him? Isn't there any honor here at all?"

"What do you mean, it's only a whale, Miss Ishida—"

He saw how the tears had drenched the heavy white gold-thread fabric of her robe. It was a terrible grief. He didn't see how he had brought it about. "Look, you're getting hysterical, let me take you back into town. Are you staying at the shipper's guest rooms at the Hilton, or what?"

"I'll be all right." She looked dreadful, but she was becoming more calm. Then she said in Japanese, "Of all the things that I have seen, so far, this is the one that has most hurt me."

"Wakaranai," said Josh, "I don't get it."

"Never mind." She obviously could not handle English now, and Josh forgot, in the distress of the moment, to show his normal linguistic chauvinism.

"I'll take you back," he said in Japanese.

Didi got up and was running ahead of them. He was still smiling. *Poor kid,* thought Josh, *he doesn't know, he doesn't know . . .* Josh tried to take her arm again.

"Leave me alone!" she rasped at him, pulled herself loose, and limped into the distance. She was beginning to weep again.

"What was all that about?" said Josh to his brother—who was out of earshot—and he started to follow him to the Hotel.

As they reached the front door, Josh realized that his life now had a purpose. Even though it was, at this stage, a ridiculously improbable one.

He would have to go to Japan.

Somehow.

I'll have to bribe one of the shippers, he thought. *But I don't have a thing to do it with!*

Looking up, he saw how the Hotel pointed at the sky, toweringly monolithic, and so dark . . . *I wonder how many stars it is eclipsing,* he wondered, as he reached the working elevator.

Chapter 4

Obasan died afterwards. Didi watched as the disposal people came to take her body from their room. Brilliant sunlight shone on the grubby bed.

Didi felt a profound sadness. But there was something else, too, a kind of death-joy; it had been like that when the whale was dying.

Two old women and a girl, professional mourners, came by the bed; they wore vivid purple and red costumes. It was a new ceremony decreed by the King of Hawaii for disposing of old people. The body was quickly stripped naked and pushed into a sack, crumpling; it was an old floursack from the old times, coarse-brown and stamped in green ink. Perhaps it was as old as she was. The three did not speak, but went about their task in a kind of slow-motion ballet.

Outside the room, a man—he had just straightened himself up, after bending down to pick up a button fallen from his tattered paramilitary uniform—started to blow a lugubrious tune on a cornet, off-time and off-key, cracking on the high notes. *Where is Josh?* thought Didi. Just then his brother came out of the bathroom and headed straight for the bed. He began rummaging underneath. Didi knew he was trying to find the bowl.

And he saw the bowl in his mind's eye: a perfect imperfection. And in his brother's eye, too: an ugly old crock. The disparity between the two visions was rather quaint; but he had long learned that people perceive nothing alike, that their perceptual cosmoses share nothing but a few semantic labels which conceal vastly different universes. Understanding this was his greatest gift.

"Oh, I found it," Josh muttered. He stood close to his brother. Didi overheard his mind: *Thank God she's dead. Now I can have the bed.* The women were singing softly, a plaintive song in unison. All the words were nonsense, just to make it sound impressive.

Didi searched their minds. They were empty. They too were dead. But their faces shone in the dazzling sunlight, like the glass beach below.

Josh was wrapping the bowl in an old rag and replacing it under the bed. It was a shame he did not see how beautiful it was . . . his perceptions were alien sometimes, almost as though he belonged to another species. Didi understood a little of why this should be so, from his mindmeld with the dying whale. It was possible for the genes of Aaaaaiookekaia to have been diluted, humanized, over the thousand millennia that whalechildren had walked among men.

Didi overheard more of his brother's thoughts. He knew that his gladness at *obasan*'s death was at least in part feigned.

The trumpet sounded again.

Outside in the corridor, children were yelling, voices were mumbling and murmuring. Today a mass funeral was planned, and afterwards a feast. The three women, lugging the sack along behind them, inched their way out of the room, stately and erect; Josh followed them quickly, and Didi, turning, saw the little lei they had left on the bed.

Like people, flowers too could be strange.

These flowers were distorted; they were overgrown and garish, like cancers, their colors leaping at him from the faded sheets. Gladly, Didi went out, shutting in the faint smell of incontinence and the painful juxtaposition of bed and flowers.

The trumpet sounded again. . . .

After a while the procession left the security of the collection of skyscrapers that was the Hilo hotel complex, winding its way inland. The glass became grittier, and now and then a clump of shrubs stood out from the crannies. Even patches of bare igneous rock showed through . . . and then dirt, as well.

Josh and the other bereaved ones were following the cart that was dragged by four yoked veggies, laden with sacksful of the dead. The unkempt trumpeter preceded them, seeming never to take a breath as the stream of angular melodies blared from his twisted instrument.

They reached the oasis, which was the only place anywhere near the city where trees grew, stunted palms.

Through the crowd and the trees, Josh could see the King of Hawaii, a stripling, a black guy, surrounded by spiders of all colors, wielding their makeshift clubs in their funny uniforms with extra arm-holes. He was on a tattered throne, an old leather armchair.

In the middle of the tree-ringed circle stood the death-shute. The large, wok-shaped funnel that led down to the recycling machines under the ground somewhere, that had been connected up from the instructions of dying computers.

An angry murmur seethed in the crowd: *Into the pit! Into the pit! Into the pit!* It was a harsh hungry sound, a savage relentless drumming. The old women began unloading the sacks from the cart and to empty them into the funnel.

His grandmother tumbled out, hopelessly bent, and splashed into the funnel. The sound was full and round; it must be a very viscous liquid, thought Josh.

The eyes of the old women were glassed over, dead. They might as well have been reconstituted out of the old floursacks. Their purple and red costumes hung limply on their shriveled bodies, garish in the sunlight.

Then the trumpet sounded again! *Why does it hurt?* thought Josh. Then: *I'm happy, I'm happy,* over and over again without conviction. His grandmother was like the old teabowl that was his only inheritance: old, meaningless. *I'm happy!* Then, shouting himself hoarse, "Into the pit! Into the pit! Into the pit!"

And after he had chanted those words for a long time, he felt somehow cleansed . . . *I'm happy!* And he was, almost.

. . . but he paused to wipe his forehead. The sun dazzled him, hammering him with the same intensity as the crowd's relentless chanting, and then he saw the girl, the sight shattering the chant-rhythm like a misplaced chord, out of the corner of his eye, having something explained to her by a kimono-clad guide. He began to inch his way towards her.

Into the pit! Into the pit!

Can she help me get to Japan? he asked himself. "Into the pit!" His throat was burning. He heard the plunk of each body as it hit the protein mush far below.

She was only a yard or two away.

"Miss Ishida—"

"WILD SPIDERS!" someone was shouting. And they were rushing into the circle, naked or crudely loinclothed, their arms flailing, their vestigial arms dangling grotesquely. They had thrown themselves on the King's bodyguards.

Pandemonium, with the old women obliviously continuing with their tasks. A glass dagger ripped one of them apart and she tumbled into the funnel with a dazed whimper.

Suddenly it was all over. The spider bodyguards had them all trussed up. The hubbub fell deathly quiet; but then the chanting began again:

Into the pit! Into the pit!

The first of the prisoners thudded against the side of the pit, yelling.

He found himself inches away from the girl. She looked at him very strangely, with horror mingled with pity.

"Quick, let's get out of here," said Josh quickly, "the crowd is out for blood, I don't know what's going to happen."

She followed him as he slipped through the trees. His hair was dripping. Roughly he took her arm. He didn't think that any of the spiders had seen them, but there might be more about, nobody knew where their hideout was or whether it was there at all. They were on the beach.

"Happens all the time, you should watch where you go," he said with a kind of strained nonchalance. "Do you think this is Japan or something?"

Ryoko looked at him with the same half-choked-back compassion. "I did not know that human beings could fall so low," she said softly. She spoke in English.

"You despise us, don't you? You think we're uncivilized, don't you?"

The girl looked out on to the sun-drenched sea.

"I don't know what to think anymore," she said in Japanese.

Her guides or companions—men without faces, in Josh's later recollection. Their elaborate clothes had shelled them effectively from his world.

"Miss Ishida—"

"You should not have ventured outside—"

The girl paid no attention to them. *Where's Didi?* Josh worried for a moment. Then he looked at the girl, saw how profoundly she had been moved.

"Why don't you leave her alone?" he said to the two attendants. "Don't you see she doesn't need to be hassled right now?"

They stood a little farther off. *Parasites,* he thought.

"Thank you," said Ryoko.

"It was nothing," he said, covering his embarrassment with mock gallantry.

She fascinated him.

For she was becoming part of his image of the new world he must find. This was no sexual thing; it was not love or desire or any simple emotion. He was looking for a country not of the dead, and Ryoko Ishida was not dead inside. She was the first person he had met who was not merely two-dimensional. So, without willing it, he had integrated her into the dream.

He had learned that what had befallen Hawaii had also happened to every other place in the whole world. He had no clear conception of the world, of course, except what he remembered from before he was ten years old.

Except Japan. . . .

"You know," he said in Japanese, for he reasoned that it might humor her, "when I asked you that question the other night, whether I could ever really go to Japan and find a job . . ."

"Yes," Ryoko said absently, "and I told you that our driver was American. But you are not American! How can a few generations change what you really are, one of the People?"

"I'm what ever I make myself," he said stubbornly.

"What *is* an American, though? . . ."

(And he cast his mind back all those years, to another world altogether. There were oaths of allegiance, ideals, democracy, things like that, but he couldn't remember what they meant. They were words that smelled of old classrooms and the pungent socky odor of broken lockers and other half-buried images that he perceived only dimly, as though through the wrong side of a one-way mirror . . .) "I'm not sure, I really don't know at all," he admitted.

"Well," Ryoko said, "can it possibly mean the things we've seen today? Are those really the things you identify with?"

(And he heard the woman wail as she splashed into the mush, the defiant, agonized yells of the spiders as they charged through the mob, the crying of strange impossible babies.)

"I guess not," he said, in English this time.

And licked the salt on his lips and felt the brinewind full in his face. And saw her suddenly as a figure from one of the *Noh* plays *obasan* often talked about. She was not an educated woman, so she had not understood the language of them, and so she had only talked of living ghosts, white-faced and stylized. From two dimensions she had become three-dimensional; but now she became a dream-person, a myth, adding a fourth. But he could not comprehend this; he was only confused by the complexity of it.

"So you are certainly not obliged to remain loyal to a concept which has certainly died," Ryoko continued. She said it not with relentless logic but with pity and a certain strength.

The two attendants began to try and attract her attention. Finally, one—the taller—said: "Miss Ishida, we must pack your belongings."

"Wait—" Josh said. "You're leaving!"

"Did you think I had come here as a colonist?" She laughed suddenly, incongruously. "I am sorry."

And then without warning he was engulfed by this completely new sensation. It was a kind of lostness, a smallness within an enormous vastness, and he saw also a whale-like image and scenes of death and peace and god-like compassion, all superimposed. He opened his mouth to speak.

Didi was standing beside them. He had come up from behind somewhere, unseen.

And somehow this new sensation was to do with Didi and the Ishida girl, and with the beached whale and with an awful lot that he couldn't understand at all. It was not exactly a joy. It was a terrible pain that assaulted him from deeper levels in himself than he had known existed.

It only lasted a few seconds.

But it was long enough for Ryoko Ishida and her two guides to have left them.

Had they communicated in some peculiar way? He had heard of stranges who could do that sort of thing. And Didi was a strange, of course. But he dismissed that at once; for types of strange were totally different from one another, and he knew what type Didi was: a *retard*.

"In any case," he said to Didi as though carrying on a conversation, "now that she's dead, you and I can start thinking about our freedom, can't we?"

The boy said nothing.

"Well, let's get out of the scorching sun."

(Tomorrow would be another day at the hostel. More children would die, more would be brought in. He would sit around joking with Mokupuni, maybe, or they would go to the nympho quarters and empty a few. Or they would throw stones at the veggies and watch them wilt. Or they would go to the art museum on the ninth floor and steal some skateboards, and then whoosh down the glass beach, whooping like children. And Didi would sit by himself in a corner and play his private little games. And he'd go to bed. And wake up.)

He watched the girl in the distance.

"I don't love you," he said.

But you have something I want.

Chapter 5

SUMMER, 2022

Her father always used the diminutive with her. "Not a word, Ryochan," he said, "not a word until I've looked my fill at the *fujisan* . . . no, no, not a word."

He took her hand to steady himself, bent to unbutton his archaic tweed overcoat because of the heat, and allowed her to lead him across the flagstoned plaza, past the grandiose, disused marble fountain into the disheveled shade of a cluster of trees. Ueno was still a comparative oasis in the clutter of Tokyo; somehow, the Great 'Quake of '89 had left it alone. There were low buildings on all sides of the square, seventy or eighty years old, which seemed not to belong to the present, but to emerge out of a transtemporal haze; moss veins had fuzzed their outlines, and the torrid sunshine would not lighten their gloom.

Ryoko noticed a big signboard to her left, where patina'd metal gates had been clumsily boarded over. It was written not in the usual Roman letters, but in the elaborate, ideographic *kanji* of the twentieth century.

Notice: Ark Project

Ueno Zoo has been closed, owing to the recent decision of the Survival Ministry to ship the animals to

an environmental reconstruction project in Kenya, East Africa.
Your patience and forbearance is craved.

Signed: Akido Ishida, Minister for Survival

"A new project, *otosan?*" she asked him, although she did not wish to talk of generalities, really; she was full of the message she must give him, and for a moment the roar of the waves was vivid in her memory, but she sensed the time was not quite ripe. Better to let her father relax, see what he had come to see, first.

They stood in front of the sign. Someone had scrawled beneath the signature, in roman letters, "I can't read this old writing!"

"Well," Ryoko laughed, "after fifteen years of Back to History, people will still be living out their Americanized fantasies of progress."

"Let's go," said her father, "it's hot, a very hot summer. The museum might be air conditioned by now . . ."

"Well, perhaps it was an immigrant," she said to herself, her eyes lingering on the sign. "It was a wise plan of your Ministry's father, to strengthen our survival by reviving our Japaneseness, to conjure up the past when there isn't much of a future."

"Oh, it didn't work, Ryochan," her father mumbled, "and the animals are all dead, in Africa."

"Everything is so beautiful now, father . . . do you remember the cherry blossoms on the drive to the park? It must be the impending world-death, heightening everything . . ."

"The mutated plague-virus got them when they arrived, we hadn't counted on it reaching Kenya from across the Atlantic so soon . . ." She saw his look of, *oh, we aren't communicating,* and that he had begun to walk—quite briskly for his age—across the street to the museum which had been, in the twentieth century, one of the world's wonders.

But before they went in he turned to her and said, diffidently, "I *am* sorry not to have seen anything of you, or talked to you, since you came back. I'm glad we can have this time together."

Ryoko suppressed a twinge of impatience, and appraised him silently in return: an old man, a wisp of a man, a small man, an unsteady man, a man of power.

They walked past interminable corridors, past listless guards with stiff hands and dead eyes, and he chattered on about this and that, so that she sensed beneath his well-schooled superficiality some unspoken disquiet.

He needs me, she thought: but he would lose face by saying so to me, a woman, his only child.

Fujisan stood by itself in a glass case. It was a brown, blotchy vessel irregularly streaked with a dull white; misshapen, crooked, by any conceivable non-Japanese aesthetics—ugly. It was—and remains—the ultimate teabowl: the supremely perfect imperfection.

When the two of them had gazed for several long moments, they were overwhelmed, close to tears.

And after, in a little coffee-shop called *The San Diego Treaty,* which served a charming synthetic coffee and had its waitresses charmingly attired in pre-war two-ply polyvinyl tunics, they each had a cup of "blue mountain"—whatever the name, it all came from the same laboratory —and Minister Ishida listened to his daughter's story. He heard the whole thing out, without interruption.

"What strikes me now is that the whale was so Japanese, he spoke about death the way a Japanese might. I'm sure he would understand *fujisan,* too, and the tea ceremony, and all the things the old *gaijin* experts found so bafflingly alien about our culture . . . father, you don't believe me."

He sipped his coffee. "Did anyone else see it? Was it not a hallucination, a dream?"

"No! . . . you don't believe me."

"Ryochan—" he lowered his voice. "Our Ministry's Back to History proclamations, the cultural revival programs, the renascence of the old life patterns . . . what do you feel about those things?"

"What does it matter, father? Oh well; these things may amuse the people. What few of them remain. I see there was another suicide wave in my absence." Then she said slowly: "Our culture has never been significantly influenced, even by the surface Americanization of the old days. I don't think what your Ministry is doing is really relevant, *otosan.*"

"Yes, your trip has made your mind clear, I think. You're right; our entire program is a cover-up. Despite our support for every form of suicide, especially the traditional forms like *seppuku,* we really are working for another kind of survival . . . and there is no way, of course, short of totally altering the environment, before the great plague takes us all."

Then with a flicker of earnestness, he continued: "So we have to find a new environment."

And I know, thought Ryoko, *what that new environment must be: the land of shadow. Honor must survive identity.* So she said, "The whale came to the right source then. He knew things I did not know."

"Yes."

"Still, you don't believe me."

"Your mother came back from Hokkaido a fortnight ago, Ryochan, your mother whom you've hardly seen since I divorced her. She has caught the plague—there isn't a town in the North without one or two cases."

Why did he not concentrate on the subject? "Father, I'm sorry," she said, not without irony. Somehow he seemed so spent, so ineffectual. But the memory of the whale was vivid to her, and she could only feel an annoyance at him for not reacting with the proper urgency. He was avoiding an answer, he did not believe her. Well then, she would withhold her sympathy.

"You don't believe me," she said, edgily.

"What choice do I have?" her father said, suddenly emotional. "How could my own child lie to make me lose face?"

Her hand was shaking. She drained her cup and set it down. Her father was paying the bill—six million yen—with a ten million credit note, and was getting up without waiting for the change.

The gulf between them was wider than all ocean.

At the corner, the chauffeur, an American immigrant, was holding open the door of the black electric Toyota.

They were silent.

They drove past immaculately desolate streets, past empty department stores and blind traffic lights, and she began to suspect him of knowing far more than he had cared to say. Why was he so unsurprised at it all?

Three months were left.

Then they would have to face the whale again, together.

Minister Ishida was thinking:

There is a little island, pushed out of the sea by a volcano, twenty, thirty years ago, several hundred kilometers north of Hokkaido. On what happens there, everything depends, everything.

(The driver took them up the ill-kept ramp on to the Shuto Overpass.) The Minister sat well back as the car rattled across cracked pavements and lumps of lichen. He felt his daughter's presence: pensive, quiet. She had grown very comely; in her classic kimono, she was almost beautiful. He loved her, though he could not bring himself to say so.

She is wise, he thought: in the old days, when they had computers and universities, she might have made a talented poetess, an observer of truths. But the sea has returned her to me a stranger, not soft as before, but strong-willed, a little alien, even. Today, she defied me, challenged my belief in her.

If she were not telling the truth, she could not have changed so much. So I believe her.

. . . I was over fifty years old when she was born. But I could swear that her thoughts and attitudes come from a more distant past than I can remember. She's so quintessentially Japanese, so much so that she doesn't understand what I mean by *survival.*

She thinks that our *survival* is really a euphemism for death, and that my Ministry, like the other two, is essentially a religion.

But why *don't* I want to die? he thought . . . like the others? Am I too Westernized to feel the need to take, in honor, the consequences of mankind's evil?

There is an island, though. . . .

His mind wandered; age was beginning to touch him at last. They had come to a cleared stretch of the Overpass, and Tokyo's clashing garishness kaleidoscoped about his eyes, even through the smog.

Not *spiritual* survival! he thought. Corporeal, factual, literal survival.

My hopes are on this island alone: this secret island, where they are building the tall spacecraft, this island from which, one day, they will burst into the sky to rendezvous with an abandoned prototype starship of the Russians, that has waited, passengerless, in orbit for forty years, to begin a journey of four thousand years, where the arrivers will have no memory of the departers, or of earth.

What could the whale want with me? He knew it must concern his project.

The intelligence of whales came as no surprise to him; but why would they take the trouble to make contact with man? It violated the purity of his image of them—for he had never seen one, nor even a photograph, and they were to him like dragons or phoenixes, creatures of dream and myth—and he was sure they were intended as creatures apart, ineffable, beyond man, living amid events and emotions as transcendent as they were incommunicable.

And now, they wanted to do something to his spaceship.

He turned to see his daughter speaking with him, but he heard nothing at all, because the silence tablet he had swallowed earlier was beginning to take effect.

Chapter 6

Noboru Shimada, captain, laughed quietly: "But you don't have anything you could pay me with!"

Josh saw his hope sink, without a trace, into the smoke-fog of the room. "I could work for you . . ."

The captain's eyes twinkled. "Don't think I'm not used to saying no, that I'll take pity on you. I *do* feel for you, but I have to suppress my sympathy. I have to survive too, you know."

He didn't seem like a Japanese. Josh felt more at ease with him than he had ever felt with anyone from Japan, in spite of just having been turned down.

The room was milky with exotic fumes. Josh knew that his euphoria was unnatural, that it was being induced by the smoke. Thousands of dollars of empty smoke.

"Look," said Shimada, "every year I come along this route. Every year thousands of people ask me if I can give them a ride. They offer everything—they offer to indenture themselves to me for life, they offer me their bodies—"

Josh tut-tutted sympathetically.

"Look, I can't allow anyone to upset my position, can

I? Japan is flooded with immigrants, it's a whole black market, there aren't enough jobs. So I made a really firm rule, Josh: nothing can buy me."

Josh laughed. "Except one thing!" He was getting quietly desperate. One part of him wanted to laugh hysterically. "I've only got one thing in the whole world. You want it?"

"What's that, eh? Your sister or something?"

"You want it?" Josh demanded. He plucked the old teabowl out from his shirt. It was still wrapped up in an old rag.

"Go on, unwrap it," he said ruefully.

The captain was crying. What was it, too many pills, the fumes getting to him, alcohol? "Hey, what's the matter, Noboru? Did I do something wrong?"

The captain clutched the bowl with trembling hands. "I—" He couldn't speak. Josh looked wildly around for a moment. Everything was as it always was, down here in the shipper's bar; the thick clouds of smoke, the raucous chatter, the old men chattering like ungreased machines, squatting on imported *tatami*. Josh watched the captain, thinking—*doctor, got to get a doctor.*

"I'll give you anything for this!" the captain whispered.

"Wha—you're crazy. It's just an old crock, my grandmother gave it to me when she died. Sentimental value —but you're *green!*"

"I want it! Don't keep me in suspense, what's your price!" He was crying like a baby, his eyes riveted to the bowl, which glistened with tears or sweat and was appallingly ugly. . . .

"You're serious," said Josh suddenly.

And he saw his chance.

"It's *temmoku,*" said the captain. "Anyone can see that. I would die now, having possessed something of such beauty." And he was radiant. *It must be something about the Japanese mind,* thought Josh, and shrugged mentally. *But I've got him in my power, or something. I can't imagine how.*

The man was beginning to cough and sneeze, and some people had begun to notice. Another Japanese came and crouched beside him, ready to carry him out; perhaps then he caught sight of what Shimada was holding in his hand, a simple bowl of black glaze still half-swathed in a dirty rag—

"Let me touch it!" the second man said.

"What's happening?" said another sailor, a white. He saw two men sobbing over some object and looked quickly away. Josh saw how his face had betrayed one moment of utter disdain before he had turned his back on them.

I don't understand this, he thought. "I want passage to Japan for me and my brother Didi," he said quickly. "And you can keep the silly old thing . . ."

"Let *me* have it!" said the second man. "I'll take you in my ship."

"I was given it first," Noboru Shimada whispered harshly, his eyes glazed by a strange compound of lust and awe.

"I must have it!" the second one shouted, and this time several faces turned around, and someone yelled "Shut up over there," in English, and a couple of people crawled over. "If I don't possess this object of supreme beauty I will die!" What the hell was going on? Josh asked himself. "Hey, what's happening?"

"Look, you decide," said someone, "it's your piece of crockery, damn it." In the background someone was lecturing learnedly about the Japanese perception of beauty and how it was alien from everybody else's.

"Well . . ." said Josh, still wondering what there was to be upset about, "I was only joking when I tried to pay the guy with it. But I suppose it should go to Noboru here, since I was talking to him first."

No sooner had he said this than the second man let out a scream of unendurable anguish, and he plucked out some kind of knife from his Japanese-style robe and stabbed himself in the stomach. He died at once, with his left hand grasping for the bowl.

It was senseless. "Look," Josh said to no one in particular, "I don't understand it at all, I think you're all crazy, will someone explain it to me please—"

Shimada had suddenly become very sober. "It was a beautiful death," he said simply. "He had seen perfection, and he died almost touching it."

"That thing—perfection?"

"I am surprised you do not understand." His speech had suddenly become very formal, very correct. He was all Japanese now, alien and full of unfathomable emotions. He had sat himself very upright against the floor cushion and was gazing at the bowl still, with a kind of serene elation that scared Josh to his very insides. "Nakamura Yoshiro," he went on, "this is an object of inestimable beauty. Look at the sublime imperfections of its black glaze. It has been molded half by man, and half by nature itself, and by the accidents of time."

Josh was all attention now. He still did not understand, but he had realized that this was the same thing his *oba-san* had talked about, in her uneducated way. So she had been right. He began to wonder what else she had been right about. If he was to go to Japan, he ought perhaps to remember more of what she had said.

"The price you ask is that I should give you and another one free passage to Japan, is that correct?"

"Yes. Me and my brother Didi."

"If the bureaucracy finds out—my ship operates, you know, under the statutes of the Ministry for Survival—I will probably be severely punished." He was very matter-of-fact about this.

"You'd risk that?"

"You stupid, ignorant *gaijin!*" said the captain. The outburst overwhelmed Josh for a moment. "I am sorry; it is not your fault but the fault of your conditioning, your environment, your being brought up in an uncivilized country . . . you have been unable of course to develop any true appreciation of beauty." Slowly the contempt evaporated from his voice. "Of course I would risk it."

"When can I leave?" Josh was too excited to pay much attention to the man's philosophical discourse, to be affected by his contempt.

"I cannot take you this trip," said the captain. "But I will be back here in about six months, weather permitting. And then I will take you. May I take the *temmoku* tea-bowl now?" He said the last sentence very humbly, as though addressing a god.

"How can I be sure?"

"Don't try my patience, you ignorant scum! How can you doubt my word? Have I no face at all?"

Josh thought: *He's obviously been driven quite insane by this thing, what with all the talk about honor and face and stuff.* "I accept your word," he said slowly.

Noboru was not really mollified. "The man who died, I don't know who he was." The body still lay there, but the crowd in the bar had stopped noticing it. "But he had genuine honor. He was lucky, to have been granted a death of such beauty. Yoshiro, I am truly jealous of him. He was my brother. And I caused him to die . . . perhaps I should kill myself too . . ."

"No!" said Josh. *I don't want to lose my chance now.*

A spiral of smoke crossed the captain's face, drifting lazily across the room. Mugs were chinking, conversation was buzzing evenly.

"He was really my brother," said the captain again. And he cradled the teabowl in his arms, tenderly and longingly, and this time when he cried it was very silent, just a noiseless trickle of teardrops that fell into the blackness of the bowl, which seemed in the strange light to be an abyss without end.

"In six months, then. I'll wait," said Josh.

As he walked away his depression began to lift. The room had been oppressive, and even the tainted air of the corridor smelled fresh. When he walked away far enough, he even began to whistle.

Soon he would leave the island.

He felt a twinge of guilt, too, because the price he had paid had also been in blood—but he expunged it cheerfully from his thoughts. And went to find his brother.

Chapter 7

AUTUMN, 2022

They are, Ryoko thought, like three pathetic old women, parasitically consumed by their glitter-heavy ceremonial robes.

Her father was there, and Kawaguchi the Minister of Comfort, and Takahashi the Minister of Ending, patron of suicides. Their oversized robes flapped against their chests and billowed out behind them with the strong wind from the sea. They were abrupt splashes of color in the ashen expanse of sand, sea and sky.

Ryoko watched them carefully, but, as was seemly for a woman, she stood some distance off, not intruding on the men.

There were some others, too, on the beach: a dirty old beach scavenger, tethering his rockety boat to a post; two little girls, kicking a rusty can; a mangy cat, sniffing among scatterings of refuse . . . but all the images were lost in the grayness, and all the sounds dispersed in the slow sussurations of the surf.

Behind her, far behind her, broken warehouses of worn concrete, a century old.

She heard them softly bickering; not indecorously, but with undertones of menace.

"Has he perhaps brought us here for no reason?" Kawaguchi asked.

The Minister of Ending, tall and sacerdotal in sacramental mitre and in purple and gold, looked steadfastly at the sand as he declared: "I have no opinion; I have come as a favor to Ishida." Clearly, this was untrue; he had come to see his colleague lose face.

"But might this not be ridiculous?" came Kawaguchi's querulous, edgy tenor.

Minister Ishida remained aloof. After all, he was the only one with anything to lose, Ryoko reminded herself.

If the whale doesn't come, thought Ryoko, my father may have to kill himself.

They waited.

Until evening fell again. Then again the water burst asunder, in the mid-distance, and the blackness loomed out of the water, distorting all perspective. The three Ministers gaped in unison. The old scavenger, gripped by terror, whimpered quietly. Only the two children were unconcerned, and went on kicking the can.

Ryoko felt a surge of tremendous love for him, and she trembled at the grace of him, creature of twilight, leaping from the dark water in a perfect poised arc that mocked gravity for a moment. There was pain, too, with his joy, this beauty made unbearable by its transience. And the bittersweet pungent wavewind swept her face, and she yearned to be like him, to live with his intensity and fierceness, a life-force battling inexorable death.

The same voice came to her, that she had heard from the ship half a year before, but amplified, like thunder and a waterfall . . . *Come! Come!* it cried.

She heard Kawaguchi's voice: "The whale does not speak, Minister Ishida."

Ishida: "Wait." The first word he had spoken.

"But I hear him!" she said.

Come! Come! the voice sang, and it was whale-singing mixed with the music of *Noh* and *Kabuki* and *Bugaku*, eerie and hypnotic, and she felt herself yielding, yielding beneath its spell, her body moving of its own volition towards the soft water. . . .

Kawaguchi was saying (she heard him only faintly) "The whale has not spoken, Minister Ishida. I think we may leave."

A shriek: "Your daughter! She'll drown!"

"But I hear him, but I hear him, but I hear him," she

screamed desperately, as the others' voices faded into the roar of the waves.

"My daughter!"

"Old man, old man, lend us your boat, quickly!"

"B-b-b-ut—"

"How dare you argue with the Minister for Survival?"

"Hai, hai, irashaimasse," a frightened old voice, remembering his place and the polite forms of address only just in time.

She gave herself into the arms of darkness. The whale's consciousness touched hers, led her into the warmth. A lone gull cried above the thunder. The water parted for her like blankets. There was no cold in the water, only a profound joy, a release from turmoil, a peace, a foretaste of death.

Hideo Takahashi did not deign to touch the oars, of course. In spite of the bewildering confusion of the situation, he could never lose his awareness of what was seemly; for he was a man of honor, above all.

They were so pathetic, those other three, sitting in the boat, more controlled than in control. Kawaguchi, the intellectual dwarf, was almost weeping as he plied his oar; the old man, a thorough underling, cringed in a corner—and Ishida, the man he had always hated from the beginning, from the University days—how well he understood Ishida. A devious man, a man with some ingenious secret, he knew, hidden in his mind. Ishida was dangerous.

But then he felt the surge of the wavewind, and he exulted. He loved the elemental drama of nature, loved the stinging of the salt in his eyes. He felt all-powerful, as though, in a way, the force and fury of it all were radiating from his strong body.

Kawaguchi was whispering: "Where is the girl? How could we possibly find her? She must be drowned, dead, we're just three old men, how can we think of rescuing her?"

"Be silent!" Ishida was grim. Takahashi saw him, how he faced the ocean steadfastly, his face inscrutable. Of all those who knew Ishida, perhaps only Takahashi understood the extent of his vulnerability . . . but he turned his attention away. He did not know whether he would survive the storm. But for now he would rejoice in the sense of power. The wind made him alive. He was stronger than the others.

Kawaguchi continued to whine. "If we die now, how can our deaths be beautiful?"

They were dazzling tiny gems, all the colors of fire, in the midst of a vast grayness. Grayness pleased Takahashi very much.

You were always the glib, skin-deep one!

Takahashi had no inkling of what this crazy odyssey in the Yokohama harbor was all about. He did not really care. He knew it could be bent into shape, into part of his great plan for the human race. He shivered with the fragile coldness of his plan, with the dark beauty of it.

The wind whipped them.

You were always the glib, skin-deep one!

The details of his plan played over and over in his mind, a black crystal absorbing all the light.

He would show the Abbot. He would show them all. He had perceived beauty in the darkness; in time they would all come to it too.

The grayness pleased him very much.

She was a tiny consciousness enveloped in vastness. She emerged, standing on the waves, buoyed up firmly by an impalpable force . . . as from an immeasurably distanced vantage point, she perceived the wetness of waves and wind, which never touched her. The mind in which she had become imbedded was a cavern, an abyss, a cathedral dome, full of compassion and mystery.

Her voice sang out the whale's thoughts.

For some moments, she struggled to regain control of her body; but she gave herself up to the joy of helplessness, like a child on a plummeting roller coaster.

". . . she's walking on the water!" a tremulous old voice. The little rowboat came into view, the three Ministers huddled together with their robes in disarray and the old scavenger now pushing the oars. It was one kilometer from the shore.

Don't be afraid, she heard herself say. A voice strangely like her own voice, but more sonorous, she realized, for she could be heard above the howlings of the winds.

I am holding up your daughter telekinetically, Minister Ishida. She is unharmed; do not be afraid.

I am sorry to possess her body in this way, but I cannot otherwise communicate with you; to find one such as Ryoko, with the clarity of perception to tune in to and comprehend even some peripheral aspects of our thoughts, was no easy task.

She saw her father stand up, even as the boat rocked wildly, to face the creature as a man should; but the others remained in a bundle together, terror-frozen.

And Takahashi had lost his composure.

"You want to claim our starship? To ask our help in leaving the planet we have made uninhabitable for your children?" Ishida said.

"Starship?" Kawaguchi stammered through his fear. "What's going on?"

What could I want with your starship? Its dimensions are wrong for me, its environment is wrong. How could a whale travel with you, in a voyage of generations?

The other two Ministers were glaring at Ryoko's father with anger and incredulity.

"Ishida, you have lied to us!" Takahashi rasped. Ryoko perceived, directly, the meanness of the man, the self-aggrandizing pettiness of him. "What is the whale talking about?"

She saw, in her father's mind, the picture of the starship in the sky, the desperate hope that he clung to, and understood him, his image of survival.

Ishida said to the whale: "We will help you; we owe it to you."

Ryoko was moved towards them, across the turbulent waves. She came like a ghost in a *Noh* play, her dry dress fluttering a little, her face chalk-white and blank, mask-like, serene.

Take the girl. Soon she will seem as if dead. Hospitalize her; remove her ovaries. You will find, in them, fertilized ova; they are my children. They are in psionic stasis, and will not begin to divide until you have arrived at the end of your journey. She carries, in her mind, instructions for your scientists, so they will know how to make them grow. We ask only for a share in your work, Minister; is it much to ask?

"No," said Ishida. "But it is a great thing, and a strange one, that we should meet like this, and exchange small favors, on the verge of the great Ending."

"Ishida!" gasped Takahashi. "You are polluting the

purity of the Ending, destroying honor! Have you no Japaneseness in you at all?"

Softly, Ishida said: "Perhaps honor is only earthbound. I do not think it will matter to the stars."

Kawaguchi: "I shall die, though, when I have done my duty. I am not a coward; and your scheme will fail."

Bitterly, Ishida turned to Takahashi: "And when do *you* plan to die? Are you not Minister of Ending?"

Stiffly: "I remain as long as possible, sacrificing my honor for those who want death, to facilitate their passage into beauty."

Ishida laughed quietly, without rancor.

Help the girl into the boat, she heard herself say. She reached out with her arms, of her own accord, and clutched her father's hands—how dry, how papery-alien! something inside her whispered—and was eased onto the boat. They were all cramped together. Hardness of wood, she thought. Wet splinters against my hands.

The other two Ministers were protesting in their own ways. "A hoax," said Kawaguchi, "there's been no spaceship research for fifty years!"

"Man isn't supposed to overreach himself," Takahashi growled, "you're violating the purity of Ending. Haven't you learnt anything at all from our past? You're tampering with truth, trying to find loopholes in it that can't exist . . ."

Ryoko felt her father's disregard for them. He was looking only at her, wonderingly, the way he had gazed at *fujisan* in the museum, with awe.

Her voice said: *You are wondering why I ask you these things. Perhaps you imagine me some great ancient of the waters, able to communicate with you from the supreme wisdom of my old age.*

You delude yourselves, if so; I am a young whale. Were I as ancient as that, I would not seek you out. Perhaps I am a deviant. But I have not yet learnt to love death; my request is not necessarily that of the others.

Look!

The wind subsided. The not-quite-night became clear. Misted in distance, great whales clove the air in a frenzied dancing. There were a hundred of them, perhaps more, and they were leaping in unison and falling, slowly, in intricate symmetries, to crash, heavy, against the water.

Ryoko felt their surging ecstasy, and how the others

were feeling it too. The whales seemed near and far, outside concepts of dimension, as she perceived them from her perspective of immensity.

It is the death-dance. It has always been said that men will never see it. Nevertheless, Ending draws near, the rules are changed.

They leapt and then they died, some of them, from sheer exhaustion, and Ryoko touched the edge of the extinguishing of a gigantic consciousness, how they were released from life, how they were all compassion, like Buddhas. The air rang with strange music, *Gagaku* music, apprehended neither as motion or stasis . . . dead bodies slapped against the sea.

See them. Hear them. They will never communicate with you. They are in love with death, and their lives have become pure music.

As though from a great height she could peer into the others' minds, and she saw her father's wary exaltation, Kawaguchi's grudging acceptance, and the untouchable darkness that was the soul of Takahashi, Minister of Ending. There was the mind of the old man, too: small, frail, timid.

Her mind soared! And dashed against the water! And leapt again, again, again, leapt with an insatiable longing to tumble into singing darkness!

But the images faded. The deathdance was far out, beyond the horizon, but its reality had reached them through the mind of the whale. And now he had disappeared beneath the water.

Takahashi, seeing him gone, spoke more boldly: "Why do you believe that we will do you favors? Is it not human nature to be treacherous?"

Then the voice of the young girl revealed the secret, that had never been spoken since speech began. . . .

We have no names—the concept is alien to us—but there was once a great dreamer to whom we gave a name.

This is a myth that we have among us. I do not know if it is true, or if true, what level of truth it may belong to. You may accord it whatever measure of truth you feel inherent in it.

The name of the great dreamer—though she had no name, only the possibility of namehood—was Aaaaaio-okekaia, gene-changer. She dreamt a great dream, about planting her own children among the primate-sentients on the dry land. They do not think, *she reflected,* but they have the potential to be great fashioners of tools. If we could only join forces.

She summoned a thousand thousand others from all over the waters—we were millions then—and they dreamt the great dream with her, dreaming with such power that new zygotes were created. Aaaaaiookekaia struggled on to the dry land to give birth, and abandoned her children there, and most of them—the ones which survived—were in the shape and psyche of men.

Even the dreaming of a thousand thousand whales could not create a true facsimile of man. True, there were the same number of chromosomes, and they even interbred with men. But some things they could not change.

Your perception of beauty. How many times has this been commented on by the other races. With you it is instinctive: the twisted teabowls, the joy in imperfection is a legacy from us; the wails of the hichiriki *and* shakuhachi *are cries from the depths of your ancestral memories. Your joy in death, too—it is a remembrance of that leap into eternity, as when the whale in his transcendent revelation rushes with joy to meet the harpoon.*

This child Ryoko is one who has inherited most strongly the ability to communicate with us.

That is why she seems so Japanese to you, when many of your values, though you have revived them, are obsolescent.

But all *of you are children of the whales.*

She collapsed into her father's arms.

Ishida held his daughter tightly, shielding her from the wind. The old man rowed like a machine, drained by terror. The implications of the whale's revelation came to him only gradually: the Japanese people had been guilty of mass patricide.

For so heinous a transgression, there was almost no expiation.

Except the one thing that would transmute any guilt into beauty. No, there were no alternatives.

There would be no silencing Takahashi and Kawaguchi, he knew that. And for both of them, this event was a singular windfall. For they were both devoted to death: to encouraging the people to die, with honor, rather than ravaged by plague, or deformed by the caprice of mutation, into things no longer human.

Another national wave of suicides was inevitable.

And it was then, in the middle of the incredibly gray sea, that a vision from his past confronted him.

The old Abbot, falling towards the ground, his robes billowing above him, outstretched as though in blessing; and the face of serenity, peering from a blanket of cherry blossoms . . . the memory became crystalline, clear as though it had been yesterday. Yet he was only a young man then, or perhaps he was already older; everyone was young when he sat at the feet of the Abbot of the Golden Pagoda.

There had been a prophecy, he remembered. What was it? Ah yes: three points, one being that Takahashi and I would confront each other whilst involved in the first communication with an alien being.

There had always been an element of concealment in the Abbot's prophecies, he recalled. And here the surprise was that the alien being had been present all the time, waiting, for millions of years, for this moment before Ending.

The shore came nearer. Everything was gray, like an antique motion picture. His daughter's hair trailed lightly across her face, black on white. Her lips were parted, as though about to speak, and she was cold.

He looked up to Takahashi, who sat up, isolated in his private silence, amid the keening and sighing of the wind; and he wondered in what way they would be pitted against each other.

I am no match for him, he thought. He remembered how the Abbot had addressed Takahashi: *you were always the glib, skin-deep one*. But seeing him there, the epitome of old, unchanging Japan, silent and orgulous as a stage samurai, he wondered whether there were not some element of brittleness, of fragility, in him.

Something that must be broken, perhaps, in the interest of Japan.

Perhaps it is this, he thought: that I think in grays, in mixtures, but Takahashi thinks in inalienable purities. (And then he looked at his daughter again, still not daring to admit to himself the true reason for his plans for the survival of man.)

Minister Ishida's memories reached back to a time before the Millennial War, to a tutor and a schoolroom, to the lines of the immortal Basho:

mono ieba
kuchibiru samushi
aki no kaze

(When a thing is spoken
the lips become cold,
like the autumn wind.)

Chapter 8

WINTER, 2022/2023

Joey the preek had found Didi playing by himself in the corridor and had taken him to his color-crazy room. Didi watched the lights blinking merrily and the old toys tinkling meaninglessly, but Joey the preek eyed him very seriously.

"Look, Didi, why don't you drop all this shit about not talking? I know what you are, I've seen everything . . . what the hell, I *know* you're not going to say anything anyway."

Didi had often wondered why it was he who had been cursed with his peculiar affliction.

A holographic rock band pranced around the table with all the mystic power of its ancientness, moving with a strobe-jerky ritual splendor. Ting-ting-ting-ting. "Didi, I'm going to let you read my mind, I'm going to show you directly, instead of just telling you. I know you can see into my mind, but you can't see very well unless I help you, or you exert yourself. So look."

And suddenly Didi saw why he had been created, he saw his purpose in the grand plan that chance or destiny had created for him. He knew what he would have to do one day, how his whole life from now on was only a preparation for that single moment when he would give everything and become everything.

Didi was not pleased by this; he genuinely did want to become a normal, and thought that after a few more decades he should be able to face the trauma of life. It was the pain of being born that was most unendurable, squeezing out into the hurtful arclight, being beaten in by the terror of thousands of people, naked and unmaskable, hammering into the tender mind that knew no shield, then, to protect himself from the random thoughts of strangers . . . but he had thought to recover from this, slowly. What he saw in the preek's mind he did not expect. And it was a terrible thing.

"I know what you're feeling," said the preek. He was half cynical, half compassionate. Mostly without emotion, though, like a doll. Then he ran around the room, bashing in buttons, pushing knobs, but without anger or any palpable emotion, merely like an overwound piece of clockwork. The room began to clatter cacophonously, tinkling and buzzing and whistling and laserwhooshing and bonging and banging and the lights danced, more alive than the boy who had set them off. . . .

The preek was laughing like a comedy villain, but again curiously without feeling.

Hammers clanged onto anvils! Young boys surfed and drowned, surfed and drowned, against an impossibly yellow sand! Satellites whizzed across the dark night! Airplanes dropped bombs in the green valley! Mechanical soldiers marched like mindless robots through thickets of jungle!

"Do you like my world?" the preek shouted, and collapsed into mindless guffaws . . . but Didi pitied him.

The lights danced. *You're lost in a hall of mirrors,* he thought.

Didi saw that this particular future was immutable, for him, and that he must accept it. And so he embraced its inevitableness with an awful love, as a dying whale embraces the cold water.

A vague elapsing of time in her awareness; little else. She drifted out of her coma and she was in a cold bed, in an old room with steel-gray walls, and she felt her belly and knew that she had been drained.

Her first thought was: I'm sterile.

"When can I leave the hospital?"

She saw the nurse: tired, hard-faced, like many workers a caucasian. *An alien! After all, I am not human.*

Fragments, confused, distorted: in the cavern with the whale's mind. Spray-splashings, wind, the death-dance, the yearning for Ending. . . .

The steel-gray walls, a continuation of the grayness of the sea. . . .

The nurse picked up a swab with her chopsticks and dabbed deftly at Ryoko's arm.

"Sleep now. In a few hours they will come for you, the people from the Ministry."

Water rippling . . . waves washing her face . . . whispering. . . .

And sank, effortlessly, into slumber.

Later—she could not be sure of the time of day—she was escorted past innumerable rooms with metal doors, down escalators. A masked orderly or two would shuffle deferentially by, eyes averted.

She became aware: I am known to them all.

Four of them hustled past, wheeling a trolley. She almost recoiled. It was loaded down with corpses, piled every which way. Arms and legs stuck stiffly out, and the faces were tea-green and twisted. They were so grotesque that she could not think of them as having ever been human.

She and her guides pressed against the cold wall to let them pass. They did not smell of death, but sweet, like incense.

". . . not suicide."

"No," replied her guide. "Plague, Miss Ishida."

So it had come to Tokyo now.

Soon it would be spreading into all their homes. She wondered if her father's project would have enough time to come to fruition.

Yes, she remembered, she had messages for the scientists. Locked inside her mind. What to do when the ova reached their new home. If it was not too late.

She watched the pile of corpses, and wondered if her mother were not among them—she must by now be dead, but of course it would be impossible to recognize a plague victim.

The whale, the whale. My forefathers killed them, their own—our—very own ancestors. Ignorance cannot be considered an excuse.

Ignorance is sin. She shuddered with the shame of it. *And I'm sterile,* she thought, *just like the earth.*

Hideo Takahashi said: "I draw my essence from this teabowl, Kawaguchi. For it is man's mind alone that transmutes its ugliness, its agonized straining-to-be, into beauty. You do understand, don't you."

He withdrew his gaze for a moment, and regarded the face of his colleague. There was no beauty there, only weakness. Of the triumvirate that had ruled Japan ever since the end of the Millennial War, Kan Kawaguchi was clearly the Lepidus . . . but was he himself Antony? Or Octavian? Takahashi loved to draw parallels between the momentous events of his own life and the simpler, clearer paradigms of ancient Western history.

Fujisan glowed back at him from behind its glass case. "Isn't it ambiguous, Kawaguchi? Perhaps even Ishida, the least true of the three of us, can draw something from it; perhaps he can even draw meanings opposite to the ones that we so clearly see."

There were many in the hall in the museum at Ueno. There were casual tourists here, even in these times, when the story of the whale had become common knowledge; not everyone felt the compelling necessity to die straight away. But this could be remedied. There was talking in the hall, a soft buzzing of idle chatter; but Takahashi knew in himself that he was the only one who mattered, the only one in the hall, alone with *fujisan.*

Kawaguchi never spoke. Takahashi knew the man to be empty, that he had nothing to say. He cast him from his mind like a potter casting off the failed bowls from the kiln.

But even he is a child of the whale, he thought idly. And in his mind he tried to evoke a kind of pity for the man; but he failed. "You understand my plan, don't you?"

Kawaguchi nodded.

Each thought his own thoughts. Takahashi turned again to his meditation on the bowl. It stared at him from an unimaginable past. Giants had stalked the earth, shoguns and samurai, and there had been real evil and real good. Now he must pick his own side—good or evil: for Ending had come, intensifying the grayness of life, so that it was no longer possible to remain ambiguous.

(There are many grays in photographs, Takahashi

reflected, but on closer examination there are only black dots, all the same blackness, and white spaces. Grayness is an illusion.)

For a moment he wished he could touch it. But to do so would dilute the intensity of his yearning.

So instead, he drew himself up to his full height, pleased with the resplendence of his ceremonial robes—in the old days they had only worn them at weddings or great festivals—and tried to draw all the power out of the bowl, all the resonances of past ages . . . but Kawaguchi pulled at his sleeve.

I too am a child of the whale. And I have the Plan. The Plan will make us all one with the whale. We will become pure.

He turned to Kawaguchi.

"You will participate in the Plan?"

"Yes."

How feeble, how malleable was this man! But there would be real enemies, too, psychological, philosophical enemies. "Tonight we begin," he whispered. Tonight, at the reception in the Pavilion of Ending. And he summoned his chauffeur with a superb gesture of power.

REMEMBER YOUR ANCESTORS

blinked the neons that glittered along the Ginza. Shadowing the intersection, the Pavilion of Ending loomed above the crumbling Matsuzakaya Department Store.

"Yes, Ryochan, there have been thousands of suicides. Takahashi announced the whale's story all over the country, and when they understood what their forefathers had done, they lost face. Our whole nation, our whole race lost face. There was no self-respect left, for a Japanese to feel.

"The most popular death was leaping off a cliff into the sea. Lovers do it together, fathers and sons, old business associates . . . the immigrants are dumbfounded. They will have the country soon, I think."

REMEMBER YOUR ANCESTORS
ONLY HONOR ENDURES

A whale glittered garishly in yellow and orange lights. He's so old, Ryoko thought. She felt a new admiration for him, standing as he did for something as cowardly as survival, against the opinions of all.

It made him a hero to her, for the first time.

"Ryochan—"

"Otosan?"

"Will you go on the starship?"

"How can I?"

THE PAVILION OF ENDING
REMEMBER YOUR ANCESTORS
ONLY HONOR ENDURES
CHILDREN OF THE WHALES RETURN TO WATER
THE PAVILION OF ENDING

They were cut off by the hubbub as they stepped into the reception hall. A commotion of kimonos, stiff hairdos bobbing like buoys in the current, old tailcoats, dazzling lights from antique chandeliers. Little pieces of conversation crystallizing out of the confusion:

". . . of course, the integral serialism of the pseudo-occidental era was ultimately based on the sonorities of the Balinese gamelan . . ."

". . . read Mishima? Greatest prophet of the last century."

". . . I've planned my suicide for the cherry blossom season, it will be spectacularly beautiful, to lie dying among the fallen petals . . ."

". . . these caucasian servants have no idea of the finer points of etiquette, my dear!"

Turning to her father, she said: "Father, why is Takahashi giving this party?"

"I don't know."

They handed in their shoes and changed into slippers for the upper level, and relaxed onto floor cushions at the long tables, to be served. There was a pungent *sake,* perhaps not even synthetic; elegant, machine-carved *sashimi* in the shapes of petals and leaves.

One thing made her gasp in wonder: the porcelain seemed to be genuine *arita,* with the character *fuku* in blue glaze on white on each item. Ryoko could not imagine that there was so much antique porcelain left, after the war.

Her father was withdrawn, and she herself did not

find that she was participating in the conversations. They all turned on Endings and plague deaths.

The long tables seemed to converge against the high far wall, where the Minister of Ending sat, above the others, haughty in his gold-brocade regalia and attire. He talked to nobody, she noticed, and seemed to be walled in by silence.

It was strange how he was a man defined by the richness of his clothing. Why had he not spoken at all? She realized, with a start, that he had spoken to no one at all that evening.

A faint cry, like a gull's, cut in on her thoughts. Someone in the kitchens, she thought: a plague-death.

But just then a civil servant asked her to relate—for the hundredth time since she had come out of the hospital—the story of her encounter with the whale, and they listened to her, those around her, with the stricken awe that she had come to expect from such listeners; and their eyes glittered with envy, when she told of the whales' deathdance and deathsong, and she began herself to hear, in the cacophony of small talk, the rush and whisper of the sea.

But as she talked, she was thinking: why does my father want me to go on the spaceship? Can he not see that I am coming to a crisis, perhaps to a decision to die?

Just then, Takahashi rose. The voices died down, the clinking of glasses thinned. He began to make a speech.

"Many of you have called me a coward—" there was a sensation at this. Clearly something unusual was about to be said. "I freely admit this. I have encouraged Ending; thus far, I have not had the strength to seek it out myself.

"This is the message of the whale: it is the final revelation of Ending. It is now time for me to acknowledge the guilt of my ancestors, my own guilt. The time of Ending is here—" he was quoting his own writings now—"and we must make way, we must purify the world.

"And so I call upon all of *you*—when you have put your affairs in order, not rashly or unpremeditatedly—to follow the ancient path. Japan has ceased to be sacred. We are a nation of genocides, of patricides.

"Had you been observant, you might have noted the laser generators surrounding my table. Before the war, such holotapes as you are now watching were not uncommon, if you can remember that far back. I have already killed myself, in the traditional manner, discreetly and honorably."

He disappeared.

There was an instant babble of discussion; a sudden silence; then, breathtakingly, applause.

Chapter 9

The two Ministers were sharing an official car, going home from some diplomatic reception in the harsh twilight. The streets were quite empty, and the caucasian driver was flying through them, enjoying the sensations of speed and power, knowing full well that he was an obsolescent breed, no doubt.

"Do you remember the Moon?" Ishida said suddenly. They veered around a sharp corner, the tire squeal strangely plaintive in the near-silence.

". . . Yes." Ishida noticed a distinctly uncertain look about his colleague. They both gazed up at the darkening sky, watching the jagged glow of the shattered pieces.

"I will never forget the night when it started, Kan. Never has there been anything more beautiful than the patterns of light in the sky, on that first night."

"You talk like Takahashi!" Kawaguchi grated, an unnerving bitterness in his voice.

"I was only trying to make conversation," Ishida said mildly. They screeched around another corner; but Ishida was used to it, it was merely a symptom of the collapse of order.

"Takahashi always saw beauty in pain."

"That's true," said Ishida. "But why do you mention him constantly? All evening, at the reception, and now, while talking of other things . . ."

"It's just that he is—" and stopped himself short.

The use of the present tense interested Ishida for a moment, but he let it pass. It could not be very important.

"And what do you think of the new treaty with the forty-three kingdoms of America?" Kawaguchi asked. But there was an undertone of mocking in his voice.

"Well—"

The car halted abruptly. They had almost knocked over a man. "Where is this place? What are people doing here?" Kawaguchi said hysterically.

"He was crossing the road, sir," said the driver nonchalantly. "He's gone now."

"This is the Ginza," said Ishida suddenly. "Look, the Pavilion of Ending . . . and look, look!"

"I don't see anything."

"Out of my window, come, hurry!" Ishida was suddenly urgent, pulling his colleague roughly over to his side of the car. "I can't believe this, I can't."

Out of the gates of the Pavilion of Ending issued an endless stream of tall, mask-faced men in black samurai garb, swords glistening.

"Where are they going? Who has sent for them?" Ishida asked no one in particular. But he suddenly saw that Kawaguchi's teeth were on edge, that he was petrified with terror. "Kawaguchi, you have taken over that Ministry, you must know what is going on . . ."

"I have no idea," said Kawaguchi hotly. "We've closed the Pavilion, everything is being run from my offices at the old Gaimusho Building. I-I'll have somebody see to it—"

They never stopped coming. In the light of the shattered moons, their faces shone, metallic, uncannily identical, each a hideous parody of the noble face typified in a thousand ancient video shows, each a distorted distillation of an archetype from the dead past. . . .

"How many of them are there?" Ishida whispered, wondering.

"Driver, go on, go on!" Kawaguchi said, pushing the man who was gazing, fascinated, his hands straying from the wheel. "I must have my rest!"

They never stopped coming. The dark processional continued, moving slowly, inexorably into the distance, where it rounded a corner and was gone. And each man passed through a stray moonbeam, and when it lit up his face it was a cruel face, a hard face, sternness fashioned in metal.

"Kawaguchi," said Ishida, turning to him, "I know that you must know what is going on. I know it, I know from the way you are betraying your guilt. Tell me what it is, please, don't hide it from me. You're a weak man, Kawaguchi, I know that there is some pact between you and the dead Takahashi, isn't there?"

"Quick, drive on!" Kawaguchi finally jolted the driver from his glazed-eyed fascination. The car throbbed to life and lurched away, in the opposite direction to the procession of black samurai.

"Slow down," Ishida cried out in vain; and the line of emerging warriors never ended.

She was serving him green tea in his private tea room. He smiled frostily at her, a trifle vacantly; she knew he could not hear her, because he had taken another silence tablet that morning. So she crouched on the *tatami,* in the background, while her father sipped, alone in his private world of utter soundlessness.

After a while she slid open the *shoji.* The Rock Garden was flaked with snow, and the wind was whistling softly. She moved the *hibachi* nearer him, for the warmth.

He motioned to her. She could not help noticing how easily he tired now. If only he were not so addicted to the silence tablets! It was such an easy escape.

"Did you know?" he said, half to himself—for she would not have been heard if she had answered him—"there is a new *Kabuki* play. They are playing it all over the country; it is called *The Romance of the Young Girl and the Whale.*

"It's about a girl who meets a whale. The spirit of the whale communicates with her, all very mystical, and in the final scene the girl leaps off a cliff and dies, because there is no way to resolve the terrible love which she has grown to feel for him. . . . When they played it at Kyoto, there were busloads trundling down to Lake Hamamatsu, and they found bodies everywhere for weeks afterwards."

Ryoko had not left the house for a month; she had heard no news. But the story did not surprise her. She only thought: Now they *expect* me to die.

It was to her a fulfillment, the only possible ending for the story. Her determination strengthened.

The vision was so satisfying. To plunge headlong into the wombwarmth, to drink deeply what she had only tasted before, when the waves and the whale's mind had swallowed her up. She closed her eyes, reliving the ecstacy.

"Ryochan," her father said gently, "I don't want you to die. I want you to leave on the spaceship. Beyond the atmosphere, among the stars, you may be able to begin again, without guilt."

"Oh, *otosan,*" she sighed—had he heard her? Yes, he seemed to be reacting a little. There was no knowing when the silence tablets would wear off.

"I have arranged for you to be sent to Aishima next month. They'll train you there, for the journey."

"Father—"

"You were mother to the whale children, after all. For a while you carried them in your body. You have the instructions for caring for the ova. You have the right to leave on the starship."

"Father, I'm more guilty than the others. I brought them the news of their shame. Without an inkling of this, they would not have died."

He seemed to understand her—he had heard very dimly, or else was lip-reading a little.

"How old are you now, daughter?"

"Twenty."

"I dreamt of finding you a husband, of grandchildren. I am old enough to remember a time when everyone dreamed those dreams, not dreams of expiation, not nightmares of hideous self-recrimination. You are a wise girl, but still you should obey your father."

She bowed to him, submissively, but denied his statements in her heart.

"I defied all my own ethics for this project, Ryochan. None of the volunteers are Japanese, they're all immigrants, and can't understand the peculiar agony of these decisions. And in the end, I only created this project so that I could enable you to escape the necessity of death."

It was the closest he had ever come to saying that he loved her.

"But I'm empty inside, father. I'd be dead weight, useless for a multi-generation journey."

"I know little about these things. I only found the

money, which was difficult because the people were starving and there was no one who would understand. I was very selfish about it, too. Maybe the trip won't last four thousand years, subjectively. There were so many things being discovered before the War, before we came to the Ending.

"And perhaps you won't be sterile, either: in all those years, with all the facilities and the brains aboard the starship, maybe they'll discover something. Parthenogenesis, perhaps; or how to clone you, perhaps, from a piece of tissue, so that in the end—the beginning—some part of you—of me—will be there.

"So give up your right to die, Ryochan!" he pleaded.

"No, father!" she cried out. And stopped short, realizing with a shock that she had been about to defy her own father. When he had revealed his need for her, his need to be a part of what he had helped to create. . . .

She bowed again, but remained unconvinced.

She had fallen in love with the image in the play, the virgin girl tumbling into the vastness of the sea. It was an almost sexual thing, an expression of her love for a being of total compassion, a terrible compassion beyond life. She saw herself as the playwright had seen her: an actor in a myth. A symbol. Without the death, perfection was marred.

"Father," she said, to avoid the subject, "recite me some haiku."

Her father did so. They sat beside the *hibachi,* in its puddle of warmth, and the snow in the Rock Garden became an eiderdown of white, and the wind sang sadly. He recited many poems, new and old, and mostly sad ones about winter . . . but then he came to the most famous of Basho's poems, the one that all the world used to quote, when all the world was still living, even the *gaijin,* though usually in bafflement:

furu ike ya
kawazu tobikomu

"An old pool . . . a frog jumps . . . now, cap the verse, Ryochan," her father said.

Trying to keep her voice calm, she supplied the missing line: *mizu no oto*. But her cheeks were moist.

Mizu no oto—the sound of water!

There was a roaring in her ears: the sound of wind and

of conversations and of electric Toyotas in the empty streets and the pounding of her own blood in her head, all echoes of the endless ocean.

In the morning, in the snow, beside a great rock, he was dead. It was a beautiful death; despite his lack of experience, he had killed himself most artistically, so that he and the rocks and the snow were a tableau of the utmost elegance and restraint.

Chapter 10

"Coffee?" asked the captain.

Josh was a little seasick still. They were on deck together, four or five of them, just looking at the sky. "What are those?" Josh pointed.

Flecks of white, clamoring in the blue sky . . . "Oh, just gulls," the captain said.

"Are they birds?"

The captain laughed.

"Noboru—don't laugh!"

"I am sorry," Noboru Shimada said. "But it is very pleasant to discover someone to whom the beauties of life are not commonplaces."

Josh watched the water for a long time. He had resolved never to think about Hawaii again. Hawaii was a week in the past. Childishly, he had thrown a lei into the water, and it had drifted out to sea. A good omen. The twisted flowers were his last memory of the island where he had spent his entire life.

The boat was not as big as he had imagined it; his dreams and hopes had painted it in far more vivid sizes than the reality. But he had not been prepared for the expanse of ocean, how big it was. He had no real concept of the size of things on this world.

Now the sea rocked them gently and they talked of trivial things.

"When I get back to Tokyo, I'm going to walk and walk and walk, I'm going to touch every building in the whole city," said one of them, and Josh could not imagine a city where walking could exhaust you.

He leaned out over the railings, then, leaving the others crosslegged still, sipping his coffee, which tasted strange and full. The sky was clear but for the birds . . . and they amazed him, for he had not seen any animal for twenty years, except for humans.

There was no one crowding him. He was free. There were no dead children floating in the sea. . . .

And then the image came again. He could almost see the silvery needles rising from the ocean. If only he could see past the horizon, past the curve of the earth, he could see them. And the alien music came, vivid . . . it was almost. . . .

"What's that sound?" he cried out abruptly.

The water was singing in the distance, sounds that corresponded uncannily to his vision's music.

"Oh, that," the captain grunted. "Whales." He turned to continue a thread of conversation.

"Whales?" Josh looked at the captain squatting there.

"I don't know where they come from," said Shimada. "There were never any before . . . they are very rare creatures. I don't know if they really exist actually, but we attribute the songs to them. They used to have them, though, in the old time."

Josh saw the image, and he felt a dull fear gnawing deep inside himself, as though millions of creatures were dying far away.

"You look sick," said a crewman, coming up to where he was standing.

"It's nothing," Josh lied. "I guess I still can't get used to the idea of freedom."

What was this sense of loss that came mingled with searing ecstasy? He had felt it before, he realized, startling himself. Just for a few moments, with Ryoko Ishida on the glass beach, when Didi had come up behind him; and after, too, once, watching the girl leave the Hilo Hilton. It was a new feeling to him, and one to which he could find no logical answering emotion, except an intuitive idea that it was somehow not human. Probably it was just his fear of the unknown. Because, hideous though his old world had been, at least he had known how to survive in it, even saddled with a carping grandmother and an idiot brother.

Quietly, the waves danced. He had been standing longer than he thought; everyone had gone inside and he was alone, except for Didi who didn't really count, and dusk was falling with an almost visible swiftness. *I've spent my whole life wanting to get to someplace else,* he thought; he allowed himself the luxury of thinking in English, since he knew he would be using it only rarely from now on. *I hope this place is it.*

The breeze felt brinier than on the beach at home.

. . . silvery needles. . . .

Why was this picture haunting him?

I'm free, he thought, perhaps not really understanding what he was saying. The sea sang to him.

Although Didi appeared to be watching his brother, he hardly perceived him or the warm, wet wood of the deck or the gathering twilight that turned the water into wine. For far, far in the distance, he felt the whales, dancing, and he knew what a secret thing it was and how he was spying on them, a chance bystander with the gift of sight.

In that far distance the water thundered and crashed. He felt his brother's uneasiness, too. His brother did have something of his genetic heritage, then; or else he would have felt nothing at all. He perceived the uneasiness of the others, too; that was why they had all left the deck and gone below. They did not understand either; but they could feel the power of the whalethoughts, bursting through the mindbarriers, even at this distance.

They shook the air in a frenzied dancing. They sang, in unison, a kind of hymn of joy and death. Didi could almost make out the words, each word a brief signal with multiple layers, a complex construct quite alien to human conceptualizations.

Here, the ocean was calm, though.

Didi wanted to break through his body, to leap into the sea, so attuned was he to the mystery of the whales. There was such peace in the roar of broken breakers and the harsh slapping of flesh on water. He wanted to run out into the sea, to imagine himself walking on water while all the while sinking into oblivion. . . .

And he almost spoke, but in the true speech, not the speech of humans . . . the word was almost on his lips. He struggled to speak it, to call to his brothers, to say out loud. . . .

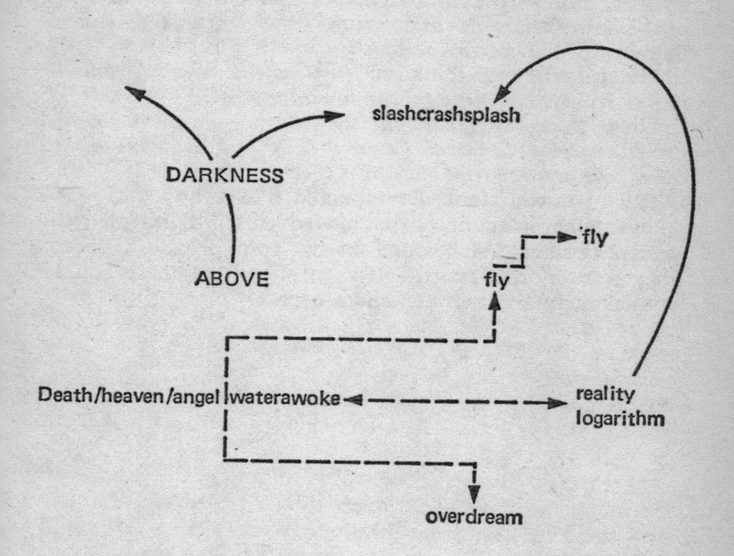

but of course he did not have the right physical equipment to make the sounds.

It was the first word of true speech he had ever mastered, even though he had first heard the call from beyond the horizon twenty years before, on the day he had been released from the womb of earth.

Unable to say it, he heard it in his mind over and over again, exulting in its rightness. It was so concise and beautiful, not like a human word at all. It had depth, like the ocean itself.

He rushed over to the railings and clung to them, straining as though to reach out to where they were dancing the deathdance. The wind swept his face and there was no wind. Waves splashed against him, whale-tall waves, and the sea was calm. Light leapt between his eyes, and it was nightfall.

And finally, when he had had so much of beauty that he felt almost ready to die, he broke the connection quickly, concentrating the hurt into as tiny a moment as he could.

The thoughts of the others leaked into his mind: his brother, still perplexed by images and emotions he had not known existed; and from downstairs, the small thoughts of the crewmen.

The captain was thinking: *Just now I almost wanted to kill myself. Is it time for me to end my life?*

They stood together in the warm darkness. Didi thought: *How isolated we are, Josh and I, from each other. We are opposite ends of a spectrum.*

The man who looked and acted like a boy and was really neither man nor child moved closer to his all too human brother. Each stood in his own private silence. They were worlds apart. It was strange, that there could be this much love, between aliens even.

Chapter 11

SPRING, 2023

Kan Kawaguchi decided to walk home from his colleague's funeral. The face of Ishida's daughter, full of some grim determination he could not make out, unnerved him; so did the terrible servility with which all the officials were now deferring to him, the only survivor of the famous triumvirate.

Climbing the steep hill, with its narrow dust-road bordered by a high wall in the Meguro district, he took in the appalling devastation without any emotion. For he was, above all, a pragmatist. The Ministry of Comfort did not deal with Life or Death, as did the other two; it dealt with comfortable aphorisms, with people getting used to concepts, with ambiguity and high-sounding platitude. Kan Kawaguchi was at home with this; for he had never, in his life, seen fit to hold an opinion. There were too many opposing arguments to opinions.

The path was strewn with cherry petals.

But there were old people, emaciated, green with the plague-death, lying on the road too. The composition of the sickly green and the heartbreakingly lovely pink was an artistic masterpiece; some ancient should have glazed those colors onto a teabowl.

Kawaguchi did not walk quickly. He took his time, drinking in the glory of the spring. For he was not as artless or tedious a character as he often liked to seem. He understood his weaknesses, and had come to terms with them. He had been a useful wedge between the two of them. Now they were dead.

(At least I have to think in those terms, he reminded himself.)

He was quite out of breath by the time he reached the hilltop. Little wooden houses were packed together. Even a Minister possessed no luxuries.

He wondered what he would do next.

Idly, he considered raising someone up to be successor to the dead Takahashi and Ishida, but he knew that their Ministries did not need any figureheads to continue operating in their inexorable, bureaucratic way just as before.

Perhaps he should recreate the Emperor—that would be a potent symbol.

The door creaked open.

It was so dark that it was a long while before he recognized the metallic face of the black samurai, standing in the room, looking wordlessly at him, waiting.

"Why have you come?" He was puzzled.

"To take you to your master," said the black samurai abruptly. "Follow."

The child shrieked once in an extremity of terror. But the sword sliced him cleanly in two, killing his cry.

On the hills, houses burned in the broken moonlight.

The boy in the tree saw the faces. Metal faces. Faces that dazzled in the darkness, reflected light from the flaming houses. Blackness that swished around them, black robes, black costumes like grotesque television villains, blackness melding into the blackness of the forest of stunted trees.

The boy didn't breathe.

He saw them swing onto black horses that whinnied and reared. They were mounted now, high as he was. One harsh face came inches away from his own, sending him ducking further into the prickling thickness. But he had gazed into the eyes. He knew them for men, not machines.

With guttural shouts they thundered into the darkness, past the disused roller coaster, splashing through the half-dry log ride, vaulting over the low walls of the amusement park that gleamed from under the tangle of wild vegetation . . . quick as a whisper, they were gone.

The boy reached with his left hand for his kite. Cautiously he tested the branch, put his full weight on it, and jumped down to the ground. It was still bright, even though clouds obscured the moonlets now.

The boy ran home, weeping so hard that the burning houses blurred into an underwater fairyland. . . .

It was a very different voyage.

The boat was similar to the one she had first sailed in, perhaps the same one; there were the sails, the bare wooden decks, the nights silent and bleak. She would stand beside the railings as she had done before. More at night than in the daytime, though, and she more alone than ever before, because she had turned her back on the concrete world and stepped forward into the cosmos of the about-to-die. A world rarefied and crystalline, untainted by the sublunary, untouched and still. The people and the boat and the sea and the sky blurred before the beckoning siren of release.

I am in love with death, she told herself. And thought of the deathdance of the hundred whales.

A night came when she felt herself ready. She rose and stood, naked to expose her shame, by the prow, where the railings were knee-high. Wisps of fog caressed her nudity.

When the fog cleared, the half-moon lit up her face so that it gleamed with an actor's powdery whiteness. She thought of her remote ancestors, shadowdark and warm under the water.

For a while she half-expected the whale to come, to see her triumphant leap, to share her one moment of supreme beauty. He did not.

She whispered, "I do love you, father," to her own father and to countless fathers and back to the parents of Aaaaaiookekaia the greatest dreamer of all.

She steadied herself to jump, a trifle self-consciously, and her eyes were caught by

. . . stars glittering on the black water, alien, but the dots in the water were so near that she could have touched them with wet hands. . . .

. . . and she jerked up her head, then, and saw them in

the sky, cold, pointed metaphors of the unattainable. . . .

. . . and knew that she had lied to herself.

She had made herself play a role, a role written by a playwright she had never known. She realized that she did not want to drown among the stars, but to walk among them.

The new longing was an ache, without any joy at all. There was no ecstasy, but only terror and awesome desire.

And it had come from finally understanding her father.

She had not been in love with death, but only with herself. And now she would leap still, but into an ocean more unknown, and truly endless.

Land was at the limit of her vision. Glimmering above the black needles that were trees, there were tiny sticks of silver that were the first stage in a journey to the unimaginable. And seagulls, circling the rocks.

For, of course, this was the voyage's purpose: to bring her and the other volunteers to the island Aishima, where the rockets awaited them.

And for that one night, before the preparations and the strenuous training were to begin, with the unearthly music of the sea to lull her, she was free to sleep the sleep of the dead.

Part Two

CHERRY BLOSSOMS

Haru no umi
hinemosu notari
notari kana

(The sea in spring
all day the waves rise and fall
they rise and fall.)

—Buson (1716–1783)

Chapter 12

WINTER, 2023/2024

The island was called Aishima. It was an island of black volcanic beaches and no trees, that rose from the rough water like the top of a sunken cathedral.

On the cathedral there were silvery spires of rockets, pointing skyward; these were on the north side, of course, facing away from Japan; and this was definitely symbolic. For the people on the island were renegades, entirely without honor, and it was not meet that their project should face towards the honorable country.

On the south side, the Ishida colony worked. There were rooms that had been ramshackled from waste materials, irregular rooms partitioned out of higgledy-piggledy huts that formed a cubist collage on the black coarse sand.

The meaning of Aishima is *island of love,* and this was not intended as an ironic name. For when Aishima first rose from the sea, a few years after the Millennial War, it had been a popular place for lovers to die. In those days, the volcano was still active; since Ryoko's birth there had been little activity, although it was not dormant. The island had acquired its name when General Yamate and his mistress, Kazeko Fukushita, had braved the ocean to die there. They had revealed their hopeless passion for each other in the famous "Nagoya document"—still quoted to this day—and then paddled in a decrepit fishing boat to the fuming island, then struggled to the summit, then finally leapt into the crater in an overwhelmingly aesthetic motion. All Japan knew of this.

A television crew had followed them, and the threevee coverage, while most thorough, had also been most discreet. All Japan had spied on the doomed pair; the general, past seventy, gnarled hands clutching the gnarled rocks, the girl Kazeko in her white dress stained with mud and brine. All Japan had heard their dying words.

It was the last program ever shown on the threevee, the day before the restrictions were put in force. "An appalling lack of refinement," the Prime Minister had said. It was not long after this that the triumvirate had taken over; and the new beautification of Japan had begun.

Now the island was cut off. Only one boat came every month, and that was only to bring food, and only because of the Ishida colony.

Now in one of the huts, Ryoko was watching as a silent American wheeled by a trolley lined with test-tubes. Another man followed him, awkward in his *yukata*—it was a permanent pyjama party on Aishima, since there was no one to impress with elaborate clothing—muttering to himself.

"Doctor," said Ryoko quietly.

The man—not quite portly, but graying, firm-featured—flashed a sudden smile at her. He was Nathan Doane, an American refugee whom Ryoko had known even before she had come to the island; sometimes he had come around to the house to visit her father; they had withdrawn to another room to talk about some secret matter. She understood now, of course.

Of all the workers, Ryoko felt most at ease with him; he was the only one who could really speak Japanese. The others made her uncomfortable.

"So many worries," Doane said. His Japanese was imperfect, but quite acceptable. Ryoko had ceased to notice the slurred r's and the occasional misplacement of polite and plain forms. ". . . Go ahead," he said to his attendant with the test-tube cart. His gentleness was surprising, when so many of the *gaijin* were so brash and ungainly. "A year or so left, I imagine, until we take off into the skies; figuring out the starship's position with inadequate charts that don't allow for the moon breaking up and orbital decay, and trying to work out the shorthand these Soviet manuals are in, and working out the cryptic instructions for these whale ova, and figuring out how to work the generation ship concept, how to pair off the travelers, whether to be purely eugenic-minded or whether to let everything happen naturally . . . I don't know. I don't begin to understand how the Russians had it figured out. . . .

"Ryoko, what do *you* think about?"

"Mostly my father," said Ryoko.

"Yes; you think about the past, I about the future. You Japanese always fascinate me," said Doane. "Like the way you have rationalized your desire to live, for example."

"I found out that my love for my father is more important than my love for myself. Compassion is stronger than honor. But I don't have to like it." Ryoko watched the big caucasian's face; it was perplexed for a moment. The thing that weighed on her mind most she dared not utter: that she was sterile, futile.

"Your father was the only visionary Japan ever had, in this century," Doane said.

Through the windows that were not quite right-angled, that were covered with cheap mosquito netting and did not block out the chill wind, Ryoko saw the night settling softly on the black peak of Aishima. She cast her mind back to when she had set out for the island and made the irrevocable decision not to die. All emotions, even the strongest, fade with time; even the most heartwrenching grief, even the bitterest anger.

She had not been able to think of her father, to *see* him, for a long time, ever since he had died. But now that departure was imminent—

"Perhaps I should return to Tokyo," she said to the doctor from America who was not a child of the whale. She saw him start. "Oh no, not to die," she said placatingly, "but to visit the grave of my father."

And there were other things she wanted to find out, too, before she took her leave of earth. But she told them to no one.

"I hear it's very dangerous," said Doane. "Perhaps I should not let you go; your father has left me in control of this project. I've heard terrible stories."

"We all have!" said Ryoko. "There are mysterious warriors on black horses ravaging the countryside. Takahashi has come back from the dead and appears and disappears like a ghost, urging people to die. Kawaguchi has gone mad. I've heard all those stories, when the boat comes from Sapporo every month with supplies and the seamen throw down the sacks of food, scarcely daring to look at us in our filthy shame! I don't know that we should believe those things."

All her life, she had been used to the cicadas at nightfall. Here there were none. She listened to the silence.

"I should go to my work," Nathan Doane said at length. He turned. "You know I want to find out how the forces work, the ones your whales mysteriously control. I want to do it before you leave."

It was his first indication that he would not be one of the travelers.

"Yes, I know," he said. "You are wondering about me; you think that, after all, all caucasians are motivated by self-interest, and that I would not be working here if I did not intend to leave the planet. You don't really understand us, of course." Nervously he fingered a fold of his *yukata*. "Actually I'm just too old." He laughed gruffly; Ryoko tried to penetrate the cold blue eyes, but could not. Except to see that he was tired.

There were many frictions, inevitably, between the workers on the island. As administrator, Doane's daily business was to smooth things over, and Ryoko could only sympathize. But she did not think he was making much sense.

"I've become rather Japanese, you might say," said Doane. "I came here before the war started, you know—" Ryoko did not know, for he had never talked about himself before. "I'm a theoretical physicist, not a builder of weapons, so I had to escape before they found me and used me. So you know how long I've been here. Your father found me shining shoes outside the old Okura hotel, the one that's been converted into a coffee factory. I had been doing it for ten years."

"Oh? He didn't tell me." Why was the man suddenly unburdening himself to her?

"Anyway, I've decided that, after my duty here is done, I'm going to return to the mainland and die in peace. In a million years' time you people will only start fighting again . . ."

"I rather think not, Nathan," said Ryoko. "We will have the whales . . . I think you're just depressed."

"No. I'm scared. I think it's hopeless, maybe; we don't know if we can operate the damn thing when we get there, we don't know if the four thousand year estimate is accurate or not, we don't know if Tau Ceti has any planets . . ."

"The Russians seemed to think so."

"How did they know? There used to be this huge secret installation in Siberia: radio telescopes, X-ray telescopes, a 400-inch reflector. All that's just a plain of glass now. They had this gigantic computer analyzing data from telescopes mounted on satellites and from telescopes on the moon. Where's the moon?"

(How strange, thought Ryoko, to *remember* the moon in one piece. She had seen it in picture books, in countless classic paintings, she had read of it in ancient poems.)

Ryoko said: "Come outside, Nathan, and watch the stars with me. Maybe the whales will come and give us all the answers."

Doane laughed a little, and the two of them went outside the hut. Ryoko paused to put on her clogs; Doane had of course tramped into the hut without removing his Lights were on in the hut windows, here and there; Ishida had had the foresight to install a self-sufficient electric generator on the island, and this had been wise, since nothing could be obtained from the government anymore. The island was well-stocked with valuables, too, that did not lose their worth like the ever-spiraling currency: precious metals, silence tablets and other expensive drugs, medicines. They were the only reason the monthly supply boat ever came; for outside the city of Tokyo there were almost no essential commodities besides food.

As the two of them watched the stars and the water, Ryoko found herself thinking of her father again. Again she could not conjure up a concrete image of him. She had erected a barrier around him in her mind, behind which the wound was still smarting.

The shattered moons rose above the stark peak. The stars here were so clear she felt she could almost reach up and . . . *they're ours now*, she thought. She remembered when she had first discovered that yearning in herself, to touch the stars. She was ashamed of that yearning, driving her as it did from duty and honor. The yearning was pain. She knew now that it came from the human side of her nature, just as the desire to plunge into death and joy had come from the ancestral memory of the whale . . . she understood that for the others, who were not Japanese, this yearning might be a fire, a passion; but she herself must reconcile, within herself, the conflict of being not quite human . . . and not quite whale. It was a cold yearning, for her.

If I go back to Tokyo and see my father's grave, perhaps I will be ready, she thought.

"The stars are beautiful," she said finally.

"They terrify me," said Doane, and Ryoko felt somehow that he was terribly old. "You know, your father and I used to—"

—and I can find out answers to the other things that have been troubling me. For instance, who is ruling Japan? Nobody knows, it seems. I would not like to leave before I find out. The story that Takahashi's ghost has appeared all over the country, for instance; that's unnerving.

"Your father and I used to take tea in the rock garden, sometimes, and he would outline his great plan to me. The moon would be full . . ."

—Kan Kawaguchi is entirely treacherous; he has nothing. Even Takahashi had a strength, a unity of thought. I glimpsed it when the whale was controlling my mind.

"We would watch the moon together. Your father told me a great deal about the Japanese mind. He was more capable of objective observation than any other man I had known; he could comment on his own culture, its weakness as well as its strength, as though he were a *gaijin* commentator . . ."

Ryoko began to listen to Doane again. She felt closer to him, a foreigner and perhaps an alien, than she had ever felt to anyone except her father. But another part of her said: *You're just substituting him for your father.* And then she reminded herself: *I'm sterile.*

"Once, your father said to me: 'the sea is dying now, but it still sings. That's what people are thinking of, when they commit suicide, how beautifully they can die.' I wonder what he was thinking about when he killed himself."

"Please," said Ryoko, pained beyond endurance. "Don't talk about him. It makes me feel guilty and proud and hurt . . . he conceived the Ishida plan only for my sake, you know. And I never understood until I was half-way to drowning myself in the sea."

"So I think," Doane went on (had he heard her? Ryoko wondered) "that the broken moon is perhaps a visible symbol of man's fall from grace . . ." (*He thinks almost like a Japanese, sometimes,* Ryoko thought.)

—and anyway, if I am to leave this planet it will be quite a bit like dying, she thought. *And if I am to die I would like to look at* fujisan *for one final time.*

Nathan Doane took a long look at the girl who had become so important an image in the mythology of a dying people, and yet was still young. "Yes," he said, reading her with surprising accuracy, "you must learn to live with your own sense of futility, before you go with the ship into some unimaginable future. I agree with you. You must go back to Tokyo."

Talking to the man was like trying to piece a puzzle together from a random array of puzzle fragments.

And then—

The night sky was alive with soundless fireworks, white streaks of light that burst in all directions from the zenith! "Is that a meteor shower?" said Ryoko. The streaks flared up and trailed into blackness, hundreds of them in a dazzling confusion, stealing the limelight from the broken moon.

"Oh, that's one of the new sights of our century, my dear child; old fragments of moon debris crashing into the atmosphere, more brilliant and numerous than any meteor shower."

"Do you think . . . one day, part of the moon will fall on us? Perhaps kill us all?"

"Why, nobody's had time to work on the mathematics of it."

Above their heads, light-flashes whizzed and fizzled out, and Ryoko half-expected that there would be squirts of sound, like laserguns in old science fiction films . . . noiseless, they were eerie and ghostlike.

"In my country we had fireworks like that, on the Fourth of July, and everyone talked about freedom and things," said Doane.

In a few days the boat would come, and Ryoko could depart. Having made the decision, and ascertained that there was nothing more she needed to learn on the island before the actual takeoff, she was suddenly afraid.

Of course she was afraid of what was to come. As humans or whale-humans go, she was only moderately brave. She was afraid of what she might learn, of what Japan must be sinking into under the rule of the colorless Kawaguchi. She was afraid, desperately afraid, of the coming voyage. She was the only Japanese person who was making the trip, and she was among creatures whose similarity of form often hid an impenetrable àlienness. The recruitment program, clandestine at best, actively suppressed, she knew, by the present government, had not provided any other volunteers of her race.

So she was afraid of being alone, of dying in space alone among aliens, without the possibility of giving birth to more of her kind.

Most of all she was afraid to lose her fear.

Chapter 13

The Abbot of the Golden Pagoda and Josh Nakamura and Didi were watching the strands of flame as they clove the dense fabric of darkness, from the top balcony of the Pagoda that overlooked the black lake, rimmed with thin snow.

"Pre-echoes of the end," the Abbot mused. "Know what a pre-echo is? Something people used to hear on gramophone records . . . know what a gramophone record is? Our monastery is the guardian of such rare knowledge of the past."

Then, more sternly, he said, "Well, Yoshiro, have you swept the steps?"

Josh was wiping the old diving board. "Yes, Abbot," he said automatically. The diving board was a relic from the twentieth century, already extremely holy by virtue of its having predated the Millennial War and being a token of an old Abbot's springtime suicide.

Meteors swarmed above. Pre-echoes or otherwise, pretty or otherwise, he didn't care for them, or for the cold, or for the Abbot's ramblings.

The cherry trees were dark and barren, below by the lake.

"Don't you smell something burning?" said Josh suddenly. He started up, disturbed by a faint odor almost like burning flesh.

The Abbot took a sharp sniff, then explained: "There's a *bon-odori* in the village. It's probably just someone having fun, enjoying the festival. But there was a kind of studied evenness in his voice.

Could he be lying?

By the lake, Josh stood within the very heart of stillness, but—

Across the lake, where the flimsy paper houses stood

Fire.

"Abbot, Abbot, the village is on fire!" He whipped around to see his brother playing calmly in the shadow where the steps started. There were screams of agony, but distanced, as far in space as the night of the broken moons in time . . . *I'm not happy here, after all,* Josh thought. Then, "I've got to go down and see."

The Abbot's composure grated on him so much!

"I'm going down to the village, will you excuse me from work for a moment?"

"You are free," said the Abbot. His speech concealed more than it revealed, Josh thought. "I will look after the child until you come back."

Josh ran down the stairs, butting an unexpected turn, hard, into the night; his bare feet smarted from the gravel; he came upon the village. He was choking. White fumes streamed from everywhere.

He was on Kamiosakidori, the main street, and there was the gutted corpse of an old man in his *yukata,* crouched over a disused fountain. . . .

"What's happening?" he shouted. He was alone amid the hiss of the spurting flames. "What's happening?" the fire answered. He was so far from a home that wasn't even home.

He stumbled to the nearest little house and battered down the *shoji*. . . .

Four old people and a child in their best clothes, in the four corners of a perfect pentagon, kneeling quite still—

Store manikins?

. . . one was breathing.

Josh stopped himself from raising his voice. Their silence was sanctified, a precarious poise and counterpoise of still beauty; *he* felt it even, after only a few months in Japan.

"Please," his voice cracked, "I don't understand why you people are sitting here; what is happening, please, why is the village burning?"

The old man nearest him quivered a little, and a single tear fell on his cheek. He reached out his hand to the old man's face and almost touched it, but drew back, fearful of its stillness.

Outside the wind roared, and the fire.

He knelt down beside the child. The clothes were wedding garments, surely; made for some relative, the oversized *kimono* pale blue with gaudy swallows and phoenixes, life-sized, swarming across stylized clouds, the *obi* deep purple and threaded with gold.

The old man's one tear was still there, glistening like a crystal.

"Please, please talk to me." And behind him the flames roared. (These were very special clothes . . .) He recognized one of the women suddenly. She was the *okusan* of the village fishmonger.

"Why are you sitting here, why have you set fire to your own village, or who has done this? What are you waiting for?" He began to shout now, but there was no response except the terrifying stillness. "Where the others?" . . . there must be others. Josh sprang up, his foot thudding against the immaculately polished wood, and stepped out into the night. There was still snow in the streets, despite the heat.

He heard a soft regular beating, a slight tremor of the ground perhaps. It couldn't be his own heartbeat. No, it was getting louder. Josh ducked behind the fountain. He squashed himself down small. Terror hit him, an unreasoning terror. . . .

They were hoofbeats, a regal rumble like far thunder. He suppressed an involuntary cry, then squashed himself down still further. They came nearer. From his vantage point he could only see dust and black hooves, thudding against the pavement. *Horses!* In the few months he had been in Japan Josh had hardly seen any animals at all, but there were a score or more of them. He gagged. The dryness blew in his face, and an acrid animal odor.

"Ai!" a terrible shout, and the horde stopped with a mechanical, disciplined suddenness. The one near him was pawing the ground. Nothing terrified him more than the animals.

Steel clanked. He saw the bottoms of samurai skirts,

the bottoms of intricate scabbards glittering in the firelight.

They crossed the street, a dozen or so of them. When they were far enough, and one turned around, he saw that they had no faces, only a silver blankness.

Who were they?

Josh didn't breathe, even. Commands were exchanged between the black samurai, muffled and metallic. One of them ripped down the *shoji* of the house Josh had just been inside.

They were still sitting there, Josh saw; from his vantage point they were small and fragile, like the clay dolls that the young girls brought down from the shelves on Girls' Day.

Josh peered over the fountain a little. The leader's sword leapt in the light, already red. The four people in their death robes moved not at all, but snapped like dolls, whimperless, as though they had never had life.

"Burn the house."

The flames twisted and hissed, and the horses thundered on into the town. . . .

Josh wasn't terrified anymore. The whole thing did not relate to any sort of reality he could identify with. After a while, he got up, a trifle shaky, and walked back to the pagoda, past the patches of red on the snow that had become a gooey mush.

He thought: I don't know what is happening here. I'm eating better, I should be happier here, it's what I wanted for me and Didi . . . *but the people are so alien.*

How could they have sat there, just waiting to be killed? When I crossed the sea I really crossed over into another universe. . . .

Then he remembered how they looked, how their eyes were: not exactly dead, but beyond life, almost beautiful. And for a moment he almost saw their viewpoint, and he was tempted by it.

He reached the pagoda.

The steps were creaking, the only sound in the night. Finally he reached the roof.

"There you are," said the Abbot calmly.

And Josh exploded with rage. "You *knew* what was going on there! Didn't you warn the villagers?"

"Son . . . you are not one of us."

"I'm tired of hearing that phrase! Ever since I've come here, you've made me an outsider. I'm human, Abbot!

I'm even a *Japanese* human! What makes things so different?"

The Abbot said nothing. He merely turned, picked up and lit an oil-lamp that had been hidden under the diving board, and set it up on the board so that it cast a weak flickering light in their faces. Didi ran over from the shadows where he had been playing and knelt by the orange light.

The lack of reaction from the Abbot enraged Josh still more. "It's as if you weren't humans at all!" he shouted.

The Abbot said (there was no rancor, no bitterness) "Listen. It is you who are no true man. For you there *is* a way, a coward's way. I shame myself even to tell you of these things, but my duty is to be compassionate."

Josh stared at him. "I know you are unhappy," said the Abbot, "and that it is something to do with your past, in America before you were returned home. You have not grown up like a man, but like a *gaijin*. You do not want to accept that the End is upon us; you would rather fight, like a reckless fool, not even comprehending the transcendent beauty of that inevitability.

"Well, I promised you a way." The Abbot paused almost as though in pain. When he continued it was in a more peremptory voice, as though he were reciting an exposition in a *Noh*-play. "Before he committed *seppuku,* former Minister Ishida created a plan for escaping from the world entirely. The Russians had abandoned a prototype starship in orbit before the Millennial War; there are no, of course, no Russians to speak of—"

Ishida! thought Josh. *I know that name.*

"The Russians were planning to leave our world in search of another, if the war proved it necessary. Since they were not Japanese, their faulty reasoning could be forgiven them. Ishida had rockets built, government funds diverted . . . and it is said that somewhere, on an island somewhere off the Northern coast, the rockets are being readied."

"But why isn't everybody lining up to go on them? Why isn't everybody jumping for a chance to escape?"

"Fool!" The Abbot's face was set into mask-lines; he was a *Noh*-personage now, not a person. Josh looked up at the night sky. There were stars there. He had never really thought of the stars before. But he had already traversed one universe, and he could not really imagine one any greater. An ancient yearning rose in him, a sly tug from deep in his unconscious. *I must be dreaming,* he thought. *Only a few months here, where it's safe, and already you want to move on, and you don't even know if it's real yet.*

"Aren't the stars . . . just lights, unimaginably far?" said Josh. But he knew better; he had heard stories. If it hadn't been for the war, men would have started sooner, perhaps.

The Abbot said: "I do not think you should stay here and watch for the end, like the others do. We wait for the black samurai to come, since they provide at least some measure of honor for those without the supreme love of beauty, who would terminate themselves . . . you did not ask me about them, Josh."

"We had raiders on Hawaii. They were grotesque; spiders and things, mutants actually."

"Fool, unfortunate boy!" Josh flinched at being treated like a child, although he should be used to it by now; the Japanese were always doing it to him. "We are a people without face. Have you not noticed that the black samurai have no faces? It is the matter of the whales that has made us a faceless people . . ."

"What are you talking about?" Josh demanded. He had heard *something* about the whales, that Ryoko Ishida had been somehow involved, that a lot of people had committed suicide over them.

"We are all patricides. We have no shame." The Abbot's voice cracked. The edge of a deep hopelessness touched Josh. "But it is different for you; you grew up abroad, you have acquired an alienness, a kind of freedom from responsibility and honor . . . listen. There is a *gaijin* by the name of—I don't know his English name, but they call him Toda, Shinichi Toda, he was adopted by a Japanese family—in Tokyo."

"Edo," Josh supplied involuntarily. The Government had changed the name of the capital city to conform with the Back to History movement.

The Abbot was scribbling on a scrap of paper he had taken from his sleeve. "Here. The address. Now go."

"But who—I mean, why?"

"He is the contact for the escapers. He will be able to send you on to where they are making the rockets. Now go, please leave me, I must meditate."

"Abbot—"

"It's cold, son. We'll all go back to my cottage, you can leave in the morning."

Didi stood between them. His face was radiant in the starlight, and he smiled one of his rare smiles, as though —*He knows something,* thought Josh. *But—*

It was snowing again, without warning. In the sky, the meteors were still streaking and streaming. Josh thought: *Didi has changed; he's happier here in a way which I am not. Somehow, I feel he's at home here, and I'm not.*

And then: *Sometimes there's a presence in my head that isn't me. Could it be—?*

The boy only smiled. And laughed, a laugh as cold as the snow. The sound was clear in the silence. Snow touched the old wooden floor of the pavilion, snow settled on the memorial diving board, on the Abbot's inscrutable face.

Josh said suddenly: "Abbot, I wasn't happy where I came from. It was a tough life. I starved. My work was shameful; looking after the crippled, the grotesque. My *obasan* always talked about Japan as though it were the land of hope and promise, and I resented it; but I came because it was the last place in the world. Now there's a new place, I guess. Because here, I'm still a janitor, and I'm still unhappy. Here the people are so still and inward-looking, and I want to push and charge into other worlds, and they meet me with blank stares . . . and talk of shame. So thanks for telling me about this new world. I'm not trying to escape my rightful shame. It isn't my shame. It isn't my beautiful death, it's yours, the ones who were here all the time. Please don't feel ashamed that you told me."

He wanted to clutch the stars in his clenched fists then, to own them.

"You talk too much," said the Abbot. "Come home, we'll have seaweed soup, steaming."

"They have burnt your cottage, Abbot."

"One room or two may yet be standing."

But Josh shivered and went on shivering, through the hearty soup and through the night. And before dawn he was already outside in the snow, with his brother beside him, and no possessions at all, hunting for the direction of Edo.

Then the Abbot was there. They stood in the snow; Josh saw in the almost-twilight how lined and shadowed the Abbot's face was. He suddenly saw what a struggle it had been for the Abbot to let him go. No one would clean the Temple now, and perhaps he would soon go to seek the dead.

The snow was hard now. It crunched under his boots. The Abbot seemed about to speak, so Josh waited a second.

Finally the old man said: "I give you . . . I have nothing. I give you this ancient haiku of Basho:

Futari mishi
yuki wa kotoshi mo
furikeru ka

We two have gazed on the snow together; will the snow fall again, this year? But I do not think it will. We shall not see each other again, even should you wish it. For us, the poem is a tragedy."

And he turned and went back into the charred cottage. As Josh began to walk, an image leapt into his mind, a memory of a vision, and it was so clear it seemed to have been projected onto his mind from outside, so that he looked quickly around to see who might be there, and there was only his brother, a harmless child—

silvery needles—
a black creature thrusting from the dark—
water, water—

and the image itself was a haiku, compact and perfect and with some unfathomable meaning, until he squeezed his eyes tight and tried to make out the needles more distinctly, and then he said, with a gasp, "The silvery needles. Of course, the rockets."

And this made him peer curiously at his brother again, because the last time he had seen the image it had been with his brother present. "Didi, are you trying to say something, boy?"

The boy didn't answer.

"Come on, kid, let's start walking, it's cold, cold, cold, and we've got to go all the way to the stars!"

Chapter 14

SPRING, 2024

The bullet train sped through the crease between two rice-terraced mountains, and Ryoko had curled up by a broken window, enjoying the stream of wind. Far above, between the red patches of mountain and the green, deep-blue tiles of an old roof sparkled, ephemeral jewels of the sunlight.

She was alone in the car. Service was irregular now. No ruddy-cheeked peasant woman waddled up the aisles with baskets of fresh *sashimi* and little delicate pastries and ham *sandowichi.* The seats had never been reupholstered, not since the last century, and they were a saggy, dead green, scarred and charred.

But the view in the window was the same view that a million old haiku had sung about. The same eternal spring. They whipped past—

—cherry trees, shedding, a mist of petals fluffing in her face, making her squeal in sudden pleasure—

—women with wide hats, singing—

—a temple courtyard, a small *gaijin* child, with a kite painted with a samurai's face. . . .

The train screeched to a halt, jerking her body up. Had someone pulled the emergency cord?

"Sumimasen," the disembodied voice apologized. A woman's voice, solicitous, but with a twinge of metal. "Please descend and rest awhile in the shade of the Tem-

ple. It is much regretted that we are here required to fumigate this vehicle. Your patience and forbearance are requested, honored travelers; the journey will be resumed in but one hour."

There was no station platform. On one side, grasses and a steep hill; on the other, wooden gates of an old temple, curious stone monkeys guarding the steps.

A sign, painted on canvas and stretched across the gate: *Saru-no-ji, the monkey temple where once a thousand monkeys roamed wild. The monkeys were returned to Africa by order of the Ministry for Survival. In their memory, these stone monkeys here humbly dedicated. This donor hides his name.*

So Ryoko was forcibly reminded of her father. Now she got up and went to the door which opened automatically. A rush of wind in her face . . . she recovered her breath and her balance, and stepped down gingerly.

Were there other passengers, she wondered. Only a dozen or so, in groups, disregarding her, almost as though they knew she had come from the island of renegades. There was a stout man in a business suit, one or two old people in traditional dress: there was no one she felt she could talk to, so she walked quickly away from them and entered the temple courtyard.

There was the boy she had seen from the train, with his kite. He was running to and fro between the seven or eight cherry trees. They stood haphazardly in the atrium, almost as though they had not been planted without forethought, and they shook in the wind, raining pink on the soft ground.

"Boy," she called out.

Not looking around, the boy said "Hi," in English.

"You can't speak Japanese?"

"Immigrants. Not speak," he said in a charmingly slurred accent. Strange, how the caucasian immigrants made little effort to assimilate the language of the land . . . he had dirt on his blue hapi-coat, his mouse-brown hair was streaked and dirty, and his green eyes never looked at her . . . from the train, he had seemed lovely as an ancient lithograph. With a start, Ryoko saw the patch of green flesh on his neck, half-hidden in blue cloth, and she thought, *I hope he doesn't know. I hope he never finds out how soon he's going to die.*

"You must be careful, boy-chan. I think . . . I think . . . do you feel all right, aren't you feeling a little ill, perhaps?" *Since when had the plague come this far South?*

"Oh, it's a little chill. Don't worry about me, nice girl. I'll fly my kite a while longer, then I'll go home."

"Watch out—!"

His kite snagged just then on a roof tile. He tugged at it, but not very earnestly; and then the string snapped and it soared, far, across the face of the sun. He shrugged and finally turned to face Ryoko. She felt a twinge of pain, knowing herself to be barren as a stone.

"You have bare feet, you are too thin," she said in English, slowly.

"Oh!" the boy exclaimed. "You can *talk!*" He smiled broadly. Then, solemnly, "I have to go now. Look at the kite, see it go, it's free now."

"Aren't you sad to lose it?"

"It wasn't mine anyway."

"What do your parents do?"

"Farmers."

Ryoko suppressed an urge to hug the boy. She knew she might catch the plague from him. She stared at the kite until the sunlight brought stinging tears.

A horse neighed somewhere. A look of stark terror sprang to the child's face. He sprinted out of sight, behind a forest of statues.

Ryoko saw two men in black standing underneath a cherry tree on the opposite side of the courtyard. The sunlight was full on their faces, but there were no faces; instead there were thin silver masks, dazzling her eyes. She half cried out. They were the black samurai, of course. She had heard of them, but had not believed Kan Kawaguchi capable of such a magnificent, beautiful and twisted scheme . . . but they existed, after all.

"Ryoko Ishida!" the first one cried out. "Will you not face your shame?"

The sound was muffled but hollow, like a Shinto gong wrapped in an eiderdown.

"Should you not kneel and pray, and wait for the sword of the black samurai to fall upon you?" cried the other.

And she knew that it was no accident, then, that the train had stopped in this place. Even in death, they pursued her father: following his child, suppressing his ideas, contorting the world into one image of a beautiful ending. She had heard of the black samurai: how they scoured the villages, and all wishing to die could kneel and wait for them, and be honored by a sword-stroke from the faceless ones. Here, in the spring, with the drifting cherry-blossom clouds and the fine air and the bright sunshine, they seemed almost comic; cardboard figures from a child's samurai tale, or an ancient epic movie. She felt less fear than she knew she ought to. She came closer to them then, and said, "If I will not wait for death, then, what of it?"

(She saw the boy, in a week or so, green and contorted like kelp washed up by the sea . . .)

"Ryoko Ishida!" the black samurai declaimed. It was a ritual. "The faceless ones are sent for you. . . .

"The Master of Shikoku has called your name. . . .

"You must come to the deathland. . . ."

They spoke alternate lines. It was more and more like a cartoon, with a touch of nightmare perhaps, Ryoko thought. What kind of madness has fallen on these people?

"Shikoku, the deathland? What is that? Who is the Master of it?" she said.

The train will depart in two minutes.

The two samurai made as if to seize her. She felt a metallic grip on her shoulder, but wrested herself free and ran frantically to the train, gasping for air. They did not move until she had reached the door of her car.

Then the first one said: "Why is it that we have no faces?"

And the other replied: "We have lost face. We are the hopeless ones. Only death wipes clean."

And then a high laughter, mocking her, rose up, making her flesh creep. She collapsed into her seat . . . but two more of them were in the seat behind her. Or were they the same ones? She could not tell. They said nothing at all, and she turned her back to them, trying to ignore them.

I know they're going to follow me to Edo. Someone wants me dead! It can't be Kawaguchi, he lacks the vision for it; but who else could be running Japan?

(She saw the boy; he had come out again and was sitting under a tree. "You'll die, boy-chan," she said softly. *And if I had met you last year, I would have felt no compassion at all.* And she saw that she had changed inside, that things had acquired a deeper intenseness, as though she were no longer an observer of human nature. She wondered where the kite was now, and whether the boy was crying.)

Suddenly:

That mocking laughter . . . I recognize it!

She wished the window were not broken, for a chill had crept upon her as the bullet train hurled through the green-blue-pink of spring.

Didi and Josh walked for many weeks, past devastated fields that had been put to the torch, more parched and desolate the nearer they were to Edo. They walked past burning houses, deserted temples and charred skyscrapers. The road they walked on was a broad highway; in the twentieth century it must have been full of cars. Now they saw perhaps one a day.

As they walked the snows melted and the cherry trees blossomed, and the skies became blue . . . they slept in the open then, not bothering to look for abandoned huts. For food they could sometimes pick fruit from the trees now, so they did not have to go begging for a handful of rice and a sip of warm *sake*.

Didi found his powers increasing almost daily. The thoughts of others were no longer veiled behind gauze, but were palpable pictures. He could think things into people's heads, often; and sometimes he could almost make things move, make inanimate objects tremble. But it tired him.

He followed behind his brother most days, thinking as little as possible about the ordeal ahead, and allowing as little as possible to show in his face or behavior. Now, more than any other time, his brother must not guess his true nature . . . *I can feel fear enough for two,* thought Didi. *I am the stronger.*

It was high spring now. They halted at a village no more than two streets wide, with one little shop and a Shinto temple, and found themselves in the middle of a *bon-odori*.

"Look, Didi! One of the temple festivals!"

The shouting came from around a street corner, and then the crowds were on them; happy people, eight boys bearing the litter of relics, cavorting down the narrow lane, girls singing and dancing the *yoi-yọi* song, a man drumming loudly, streamers flying through the air . . . Josh and Didi got out of the way of the procession, then they joined in. They clamored like a cloud of locusts, the people.

"Excuse me, sir, could you tell me how far we are from Edo?" Didi heard his brother ask.

. . . no one heard him. He gave up, and Didi followed him and the others to the temple. Its gates were wooden, rotten and very dirty, but someone had tied garish streamers and paper lanterns to the posts.

Yoi-yoi, the women sang, a primitive, ancient song. *Yoi-yoi.* The drums pounded through the racket. . . .

Aiiee! a scream went up through the crowd. Didi could not see what it was for a moment, then the drum pounding faltered to a stop.

Under the gates, a figure was materializing.

Didi clutched his brother's hand. . . .

A tall man, three meters high, stood in the gateway, robed in black. The crowd was instantly hushed. Like one man they knelt and made obeisance. Didi and Josh found themselves doing the same. A mist rose up from the ground, and the man began to speak.

I am Takahashi, Minister of Ending, returned from the dead as Yama, the god of Death spoken of in the Buddhist scriptures.

(Didi tried to reach the man's thoughts, but there were no thoughts at all. He felt no consciousness where the man was standing, and he panicked for a moment, thinking, *I've lost my powers.* But then he knew that it was merely a simulacrum, a projection of the kind that Joey the preek had had in his room at the Hilo Hilton . . . a product of pre-war technology. But the fear in the others was real.)

"Who is this Takahashi?" he heard Josh asking someone.

"Don't you know anything?" a young man, green in the face.

"I'm an American."

"Silence, and listen."

The ghost said: *We are all responsible for making the Ending as beautiful as possible. These are the last days, and all of us must play a little role in the final work of art. Each of us must die, so that the Ending is a perfect one.*

He spoke so quietly that you had to strain hard to catch his words. They were beautiful words; Didi saw through them an image of Ending, of empty earth and ocean, of cherry blossoms falling in a land of no men, of the grasses growing, of the world healing, dying . . . the words tempted him terribly.

I have therefore decreed that the black samurai shall come into existence and do my will. When any man is ready for death, or any woman, for honor is denied to no human being in these last days, he shall wait and pray for the sword of death to strike him.

Honor, always honor! Honor alone endures when the earth is not.

The crowd was murmuring now. Didi heard a few voices: "Takahashi is the greatest *sensei* of all . . . we should follow him . . . he died to show us the way . . . we who killed our own ancestors, we must join them now . . ." and a thousand death-wishes bombarded his mind, death-longings tainted with despair.

Why is this wrong? thought Didi. *The whales, when they die, die with a supreme joy.* And he saw that there was no hint at all of joy in these people's death-yearnings. Only a terrible hopelessness. What kind of beauty was this? And he knew that the message of the ghost was motivated only by hate.

"This is awful," said Josh suddenly. "Let's go away from here." And Didi knew that even his brother had been tempted. It was not even necessary to commit suicide in the classic way; one need only wait.

And Didi thought of a word in the true speech:

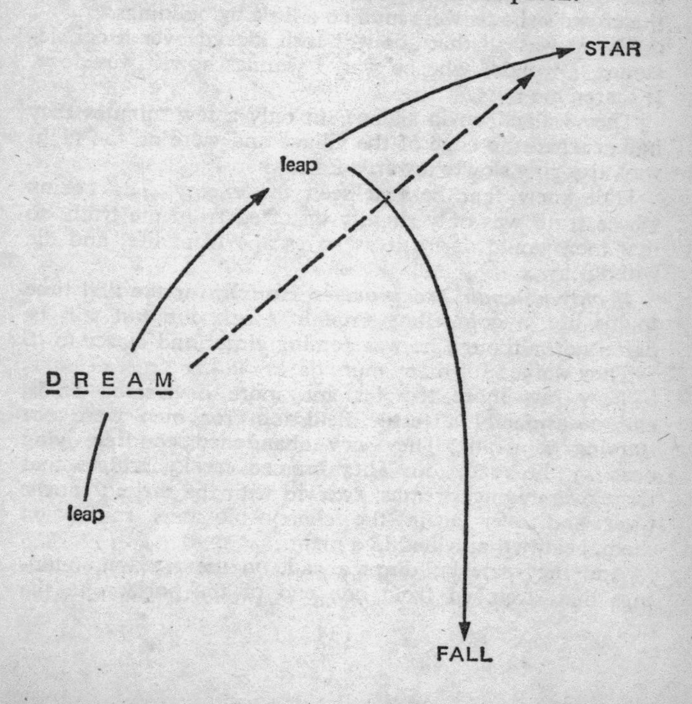

and he thought, if I could only push the air around me, make it reverberate with that word. I almost can.

And he *thought* the word as hard as he could, and put it into Josh's mind as far as Josh was able to comprehend it.

Josh said: "Didi, what are you doing to me? I can see the same scene again, the silvery needles and the island and the sea, the needles which must be rockets, Didi. Are you making me think this?"

"LET'S GO!" Didi shouted in his mind. "I CAN'T LET YOU BE EXPOSED TO ANY MORE OF THIS!"

"I guess we should go," Josh said quietly. The crowd was stirring now, and the figure under the gateway had dematerialized. The litter with the god was being hauled into the air again, and the song began softly.

Yoi-yoi—

The women in their blue-and-white *yukata* danced in a circle, as the crowd parted for them, and finally the drummer picked up his instrument and began again, at first reluctantly, then louder, more confidently . . . Josh and Didi pushed their way into a deserted alley, where the crowd's shouts were muffled a little by buildings.

"What was all that about?" Josh kicked over a cobblestone. "I wonder who he was, I wonder how it was done. It scared me a lot."

They walked on in silence. In only a few minutes they had reached the edge of the village and were on the highway, trudging slowly towards Edo.

Didi knew that he had seen the enemy. The enemy whose truth was only slightly distorted from the truth, so that men would desire it as an escape from life, and die without love.

If only he could speak out—! He felt, for the first time in his life, a compelling urge to speak out; but still he dared not, although he was coming closer and closer to it.

They walked for many more days.

They saw more temples and more devastated fields, and occasionally a fertile field too, for men were not starving to death. They saw abandoned children lying dead by the road, too. They crossed creaky bridges that went over raging streams, swollen with the melted snows. Over and over again the cherry blossoms rained on them, beauty that wilted in a night.

And they saw buildings ahead, on the horizon, buildings that stretched from one end of the horizon to the other. Pyramids upon pyramids, skyscrapers upon skyscrapers, crazy spiderwebs of highways, like old lace, and the highway broadened even more and forked off and went over and under and around them, and now and then a little car sped soundlessly over the latticework. . . .

Didi had never seen a town bigger than Hilo; he cried out involuntarily, so that his brother turned and stared at him, hard, and he caught the thought: *he understands, really,* and hastened to make himself moronic and expressionless again. . . .

They ran the last few miles. Into the crazy forest of concrete.

Chapter 15

Shikoku. Shikoku de gozaimasu.

The train's announcement, couched as it was in the obsequious speech mode, sounded curiously insincere coming from the toneless, metal voice.

The train pulled into a station that Ryoko never knew existed. A wild thought: *is this the right train?*

She opened her eyes. *Don't panic.* Out of the window, black steel gates, from which hung black draperies. Across the platform-shelter, in the open air, a solitary cherry tree.

Looking upwards from the gates:

The huge, dough-doll figure with the moving eyes that used to guard the entrance to Fuji Highland, the children's park, peered over the barbed-wire-crowned brick walls. An old roller coaster wound around behind it. Ryoko saw a lake, too, vaguely, and a few pagodas, and a squat row or two of wooden houses such as you might find in any village; and, wildly incongruously, a fifteen-or-so-story department store such as one used to find on the Ginza, full of flashing lights and advertisements.

And behind them all was Mount Fuji!

This isn't the way to Tokyo! She knew that she was

dreaming. She turned and saw that the two black samurai were still sitting behind her, wordlessly; all she could hear was a soft breathing, a quiet rasping against the metal of the masks.

As she watched them, the two men got up and moved towards the doors. They walked slowly, with the grace of *kabuki* actors; despite their comic-book attire, they appeared noble, dignified, frightening.

As the doors slid shut, Ryoko breathed deeply, relieved that they had not attempted to carry her off.

The announcement came again:

By order of the Government of Japan. All public transportation to and from the Imperial City Edo will be routed through Shikoku in order to facilitate those who desire to take the honorable way.

She looked out of the window, again. Every passenger was standing by the platform now. She must be the only one left on the plain. They were standing quietly by the gate. Their faces—the old men's, the peasants', the flaccid, business-suited ones'—they were all suffused with an awesome calmness, a peace which she desperately envied.

She knew what Shikoku was.

And she understood the meaning of Takahashi's suicide, the year before; when a hologram had eaten dinner with hundreds of guests, and the "death" had taken place quietly, off-stage. It had all been some kind of scheme. Takahashi was, above all, a consummate actor; there was no truth in him at all.

(There had been rumors that a "ghost of Takahashi" had appeared in many villages of Central Honshu, prophesying and revealing truths. How simple it was, with the old technology, to delude the peasants, brought up in ignorance. . . .

Takahashi was not dead!)

And suddenly he stood there by the gate, a small figure, in the distance, misted by artifice, welcoming the citizens of his new kingdom.

Ryoko closed her eyes, terrified.

The train pulled away, and then she opened her eyes and stared at the surreal Deathland with a strange fascination . . . everything was out of scale.

The mountain wasn't even Mount Fuji! It was not high enough, not wide enough, it was distorted. . . .

The train whipped around a curve, and the mountain

disappeared! It had been a two dimensional simulacrum, a projection nothing more at all.

Ryoko said aloud, "I've got to find him. I've got to stop this madness, for my father's sake!"

But she knew that she could not fight him alone, and that for her father's sake she must preserve herself, keep herself alive, for the sake of the stars. . . .

Knowing she was alone and that no one would see her, she buried her head in her hands and wept passionately. The wind from the window painted black streaks of hair across her face, and the rushing of the train smothered her sobs. A cherry blossom fell from her hair onto the grimy floor.

A cold wind swept through a stone courtyard. It was in the Pavilion of Ending. It littered the gray stone with pink petals, gathered from the outside. Stone lanterns stood along the sides. But there were few petals and much, much grayness. As he entered, the man shuddered; for the eaves of the rooves extended almost to the middle of the courtyard, casting it into gloom. The man walked quickly towards the small island of light and warm where the spring shone through. He hesitated a moment, then continued, into the shadow.

Kan Kawaguchi—Ruler of Japan by default—walked up to a portal where stood stone guardians grimacing, four meters tall, dwarfing the two humans who were also guarding. Silver-faced, they regarded him from their impenetrable eye-slits.

Kawaguchi saw how here and there their black tunics were flecked with a pink dandruff of cherry petals. . . .

"You may not enter!"

"The Master is composing a haiku!"

Kan Kawaguchi composed himself and addressed the two guards indignantly. "Do you not know me?" he hissed, aware that he must sound masterful, that he must live up to his rank.

"Of course we know you," said the left one. "Kan Kawaguchi, and Ruler of Japan, and of this Pavilion."

"Then admit me at once!"

Swords leapt from their scabbards, clashed in an X over the threshold.

Kawaguchi was afraid now. Was this a coup, a revolution? The man didn't dare, surely! There was the pact—

"ADMIT HIM!" a voice boomed.

"Hai!" the two guards exclaimed in unison. The swords vanished into their scabbards, and the guards wheeled smartly around to let him pass.

He was over the high threshold, taking great care not to step on it: he was superstitious, even in these modern times.

One of the Deathbound women took his shoes. Her white kimono fluttered as she made obeisance. . . .

"When is your time, Deathbound?" he asked, not looking at her directly.

"Next week, Lord." Her eyes were downcast.

"Good." He ignored her after that, and ascended two steps to a small room, a very plain tea-drinking room walled with *shoji* and with a *tatami* floor, and a low table with *chamon* ready for tea-drinking.

And was in the presence of the Death Lord.

"Kawaguchi! You are sniveling like a wounded animal. Come, some tea." The Death Lord poured, motioned Kawaguchi to squat opposite him, and called to another Deathbound woman who was waiting in a corner. "Kazu, the *shoji*, quickly."

The paper walls slid aside. Kawaguchi saw a pool, beside a rock garden, and a stone lantern overlooking it, and a wall topped by barbed wire.

"The End approaches! Soon, soon, Kawaguchi; so we must surround ourselves, more than ever, with beautiful things. Is that not the essence of the Zen experience, the *satori?* Listen to this—

Samazama no
mono omoidasu
sakura kana

So much, so much is brought to mind: cherry blossoms. Look, one has fluttered in."

"Is that the haiku you have been composing?" Kawaguchi asked. He put a touch of irony in his voice; naturally, he recognized the poem, but did not know his master's mind well enough to know whether he should admit it . . .

"Imbecile!" the other laughed, his laughter mocking and overwhelmingly belittling. Kawaguchi cringed involuntarily. "Don't you recognize one of the most famous haiku of Basho?"

"Well . . . of course, Death Lord. I was just humoring

you. You have so much to think of, with the End coming."

Death Lord spoke with a dark, guttural voice, like a character in a *Noh* play. Kawaguchi knew better than to suppose that he was insane. He knew he was facing a man he could never win against. When he dug against the man he encountered walls harder than diamonds.

"Your reports?" Death Lord asked.

"One: the work is going smoothly. Shikoku is completed and may be occupied by you at any time. A procession will be organized from Edo, in traditional *daimyo* style."

"Good. What about the Ishida project?"

"We have located Ryoko Ishida. She is on her way to Edo. She was with *them*."

"Ishida!" the man cried out, and there was pain and hatred in his voice. There at least, Kawaguchi thought, he is still human. "Give me more tea," he said, and the woman served him, unobtrusively. Then he turned to Kawaguchi, raised his tea politely and drank. "These are bad thoughts for a tea drinking," he said.

"Hai," said Kawaguchi. But he thought his own thoughts. Such as how to overthrow his master. All the while knowing how powerless he was against him.

"Well, Kan-kun, we are two old men who sit here deciding the destinies of worlds . . . and watching the cherry petals settling on the pond . . . no more tea, woman, let us have *sake*!"

The woman scuttled about, clearing away the tea-things; putting out more cups and a *sake*-flask of smooth white porcelain.

"Well, companion, speak! '*Without* sake, *what to me are cherry blossoms,*' eh? Drink with me at least." He lifted his little cup. *"Kampai."*

"Kampai," echoed the other tonelessly. He drank deeply, reveling in the smoothness of the now-rare fluid, savoring its warmth. Then he went on: "the holographic simulacra that you designed are very effective. Each day there are more and more converts. And of course, the black samurai—"

"Good, good. How many people left in Japan, then?"

"Unknown, Death Lord. But considerably reduced from last year. The touring *kabuki* companies that play *The Romance of the Young Girl and the Whale,* they are helpful too."

"It's very bad for us, that the girl still lives, then." Kawaguchi detected a yearning in his master's voice. It was the yearning of a poet, or a painter who has one brushstroke not quite right, and is considering seriously whether to rework the whole composition . . . "Perhaps, perhaps a change in the plan—"

"It must be perfect!"

"Hai."

"You fool, to ask me if the haiku of Basho were the haiku I had composed. You fool! Let me tell you about the haiku that I have composed . . ."

Kawaguchi did not look up. He buried his gaze in the *sake* cup, preparing himself for another self-aggrandizing speech.

"Kan, the entire history of the world seems like an eternity to us mortals. But in the history of the solar system, the history of the galaxy . . . it is nothing at all! you understand that? It is as short, as compressed, as elegant as a single haiku. What do the carbon-specks in the brushstrokes know of poetry, Kawaguchi?" And Kawaguchi saw in his master's eyes a kind of wild joy, like a child's at an incredible new present. "We are those motes of dust, those tiny tiny parts of a brushstroke, we with our chaotic lives! But there's a difference . . . nature is not an artist. Nature does not write haiku. Men write haiku. The world cannot end in chaos, with things running wild, with gangs running rampant, with cannibals, with dog eating dog and plague-deaths and abominable mutations. Oh, I know it is so in other countries, but we are *Japanese*. We are the children of the whale, who have committed the original sin of patricide . . . but we have pride, and we must die in beauty.

"See the difference! We—the specks of dust in this haiku—we are conscious! We can bend nature! We can force it to become beautiful. For it is the last line of the haiku that makes the other two lines significant, that illuminates the whole poem. And we have the power to shape that last line. And by doing so, we shape the whole of our history. We give it its true meaning. And we atone for our sin of killing our ancestors, because that killing has become an act of preparation for our act of supreme beauty."

I am not privileged to see this beauty, thought Kawaguchi sadly. But when he looked up at his master's face, an old face now, furrowed by worries and schemes, he could glimpse a little of it, even he.

"Hideo—" he said, stretching out his arm to touch the old man.

"Never call me by name!" grated Hideo Takahashi, Death Lord.

And Kawaguchi noticed for the first time that his master had used the word *chin* when he referred to himself; and that this word had been obsolete for over seventy years. It was the pronoun used by the Divine Emperor when speaking of himself, and had been dropped by the Emperor Hirohito after the Second World War, almost a century before . . . he wondered what that meant, whether Takahashi meant to take on, in name, what he already was, in fact.

Another thought struck him, then: for thousands of years, the pronoun *chin* had set the Emperor apart from all other people on the earth . . .

Did Takahashi mean to be so alone, so apart?

He signaled to the Deathbound to close the *shoji*. He did not wait for an order from Death Lord. Death Lord was quiet, lost in some private sorrow.

Kawaguchi thought: *By electing to use the pronoun* chin, *you have made yourself no longer a human being. Have you always wanted to be so alone?*

And Kawaguchi pitied him. And then he laughed at himself over that, pitying a man who ruled over everything in the world.

Chapter 16

There was an old house of the old style, crammed into the space between two larger ones, in Meguro District; this part of Edo was largely rubble now, abandoned. On concrete stilts the Shuto Expressway still ran overhead; but some of the road had fallen in, making heaps of rough stone on the streets below. Meguro District had escaped the house-numbering reform of twenty years before; so it was hard for Josh and his brother to find the address.

"Look," cried Josh suddenly. "It must be up this slope here, along this narrow alley." His brother watched him, then followed. He had become weaker, Josh thought, since arriving here; the euphoria of Japan had worn off. Instead his brother seemed troubled.

He watched his brother straggle up the slope. "Quick," he said. "Find the number . . ." He talked for his own benefit really. And saw the house. "Look, Didi! Here's where we're going to find the stars! . . ."

He waited for his brother for a moment. But then he could not contain himself. He charged up to the door, with the spring wind lashing him, and knocked hard with his fists.

"There's no answer," he said. Didi had come up to him. He beat harder on the old wood. Something rattled inside the house. Turning, Josh glimpsed two black silhouettes against the road, higher up, black samurai walking stiffly. Something was wrong. He smashed in the *shoji* with the palm of his hand.

The paper walls gave with a *thwack!* and they were standing inside, still wearing shoes on the bare tatami. "Toda-san . . ." Josh called out softly.

Wind had come into the house now, and the edges of the torn *shoji* fluttered.

"Toda!"

There was another room behind. Still not taking off his shoes, Josh went over, trailing mud on the tatami. *I haven't come here for nothing!* he told himself. I haven't, *this must be the way out, it must!*

He threw open the door.

It was a Western-style room, but unlike his Hilton room back on Hawaii: a little bed covered with yellow sheets, a dirty rug, and on the wall—

A poster. Against a black backdrop, an artist's impression—a space vehicle! Josh touched the shiny paper gently. He thought: *My whole life I tried to get off the island. I got off, and here I'm on another island where the people have gone crazy, where they're just waiting to be killed. It's not just another country I've been longing for! It's a whole 'nother world!* He reached out his hand to touch Didi, aware of an eerie foreboding . . . he looked around. There was a human hand on the floor, freshly severed.

He stared at it dumbly for a moment. Then—

All over the room there were little parts of a human being. An ear by the pillow on the bed. A finger by the window sill. And he recognized the smell in the room, with a start. It was a familiar smell, the smell of the Hostel for stranges, on Hawaii, the smell of dead people.

He was not afraid of dead people. How could he be, with what he had lived through? But the thorough precision of dismemberment startled him.

I've lost the stars!

Rage hit him, uncontrollable. He smashed his hands against the walls, hurting them, screaming. He had lost everything. He had no food, even. He had no home. There had been no point coming here!

He wanted to die. For the first time in his life.

But his anger was quickly spent. He understood that the black samurai must have done the killing; but surely this was not a man to submit to death. And yet, according to the theory believed in the Abbot's village, the black samurai only came for those who were already committed to death. There had been—even Josh could understand this—even an element of beauty in this . . . but here was a man who was working for survival, not death!

Something made Josh prick up his ears.

There was a quiet singing in the air. Alien voices, high-pitched cries over low hums, a music that seemed to come out of a remote remembrance, out of some ancestral past . . .

Who was singing? Only Didi was in the room, and Didi was leaning against the window, looking outside over the city . . .

It was a beautiful music. It seemed to have been plucked out of the empty air. And then it faded into the sounds of the winds. *I'm having aural hallucinations,* thought Josh. *This is getting to me.* And then: *I can't die! What would Didi do?*

When he came to himself, he decided, he and Didi would walk out again into town and beg for work, or forage like rats in the city maze. They would survive. They must forget about leaving Japan, forget that they had ever heard of the Ishida project.

Or perhaps go back to the Abbot. . . .

"Didi, let's go," he said at last.

They left the house. The fresh air was sharp, after the stench of the dead man.

Josh had never hated Japan so much. He knew they were aliens, with strange ideas and ways of life, and that he could not fight them alone. They would probably force him into the madness, force him to commit suicide like all the others.

He was helpless. Alone.

He reached the street from which the alley-slope had branched off, and picked a direction at random, and began walking very quickly, not waiting for his brother to catch up with him.

The Meguro subway station was still operational. You didn't have to pay anything; just squeeze in through the rusty turnstile, and there was a train every two hours or so. Didi got through easily; his brother gave up and climbed over the railings.

The subway station was in the basement of a twentieth-century department store which had closed only recently. They gazed through display windows underground, at manikins in fine clothes, at plastic models of exotic foods . . . there was dust in the windows. Underground, the air was stale.

They waited awhile by the platform. Occasionally the wind gusted through.

They got into an empty compartment. They were the only ones. It was the Yamanote line, the circle line; and Didi saw that Josh intended to sit, aimlessly, while the train went around and around in circles for the rest of the day.

Didi didn't know what to do next. He had seen, on Hawaii, in the preek's mind, what lay ahead in the future; but it was only a single image, and he had no idea how they could reach that point from this one in time. There seemed to be no connection between the future he had glimpsed and the death of Toda, the Ishida Colony contact.

Well, he thought: sometimes preeks do not see into the right timelines. There is choice in the future. . . .

The train started but they did not sit down. Didi saw that his brother had sunk into a quiet despair. He was without hope. And Didi, who loved and idolized his brother almost to the exclusion of everything else, was helpless too. Was this the time to speak?

But he could not speak.

They flashed through dark tunnels that were all the same, squealed to a halt at stations each as empty as the last.

Didi had been able to speak today; at least to express his sorrow in the true speech . . . he was drained by the effort.

His gift was a tragedy for him. Physically, he could never join his brothers in the ocean. He couldn't even speak the language that he understood instinctively, in all its complexity and multilayered polyphony, except by forcing the air to sing.

The tunnels went on and on. Was it day or night?

"We're getting off at the next stop," Josh said finally.

It was Ueno Park.

They walked aimlessly until they heard distant drums

and flutes, then they followed the sounds through empty streets into the Park itself, along a boulevard shaded by tall evergreens. It was twilight.

A sign read:

Under the Fountain: a special performance of The Romance of the Young Girl and the Whale, *by the Shikoku Kabuki Troupe. Each evening at dusk.*

Didi thought hard at his brother: *Go, see it! Perhaps we can learn something. . . .*

Josh said: "Come on, Didi. Perhaps we can find out something about what this madness is all about. Maybe we'll even see a solution."

The music grew louder, drowning the whispering of the trees.

Chapter 17

After Ryoko returned to her host's little house in Meguro to find that the kind caucasian had been brutally murdered, that the house had been broken into at least twice—

Clearly she could not remain in Edo any longer. Her desire to visit her father's grave, to gaze on *fujisan,* all the things she had planned to do were just dreams now. She must return to Aishima at once. Luckily, a bullet train would leave in a few days.

Ryoko decided on impulse to go back to Ueno Park. She had been there the night before and the night before that, too, watching *The Romance of the Young Girl and the Whale.* It was the weird fascination of seeing herself, so true to life and yet so falsified, that drew her every time.

The performance featured Utaemon, the greatest actor of the century, who had named himself after the greatest actor of the previous century. How low he had fallen! Acting in the open air, and the Kabuki-za and the National Theater all closed down for nearly a decade now.

Ryoko found herself one of the crowd. She was still sick from the memory of finding Toda's corpse dismembered. Now there would be no new recruits for the Ishida Colony; he had been the last of their contacts.

Dusk was settling in the square where she and her father had walked so often. With the waterless fountain for a backdrop, the play began: shrill flutes sobbed in the night air, exquisitely mournful, their long wailing melodies punctuated by sharp wood-blocks and by deep resounding drum-strokes.

Utaemon stepped from his tent-dressing room, into the circle of broken moonlight.

As always, there was a gasp from the crowd. The man was inhumanly beautiful! And he looked so much like Ryoko, not so much in the face itself, which was chalk-white with the kabuki makeup, but the little movements, the indefinables. He wore a white kimono heavily embroidered with gold thread that sometimes caught the half-light, gleaming suddenly and growing dull again. He moved, and his slow walking was a dance of utter elegance, across the flagstones.

The shamisen twanged. He moved in silence then, save for the rustling of the trees.

There stood the whale. An old man in a whale mask. And they conversed, in words that had become legend. But not the true words, the ones Ryoko remembered: words in high verse, intoned in the strange, contorted high speech.

They did not talk about spaceships or survival. They talked about love, death, and the last Ending. There was love between the Girl and the Whale, love that could never be consummated because they were aliens to one another.

(Ryoko trembled at this part, because there *had* been a profound sexual element in her longing for death. By drowning she would have given herself to the whale, and the image was powerful.)

. . . the play continued. Ryoko's interest wandered. She watched the crowd; none of the faces seemed familiar, except for two, quite near her, a man and a boy; but she could not place them. And she could have sworn that there were more black samurai there than before.

Yes. Taller than the crowd, their metal faces shone from the blanket of black hair. *They were like vultures!* Who could they be waiting for? What could they be watching for? She shivered.

Maybe I should have hidden away somewhere tonight.

Everything happened all at once. Black samurai surrounded her, reaching for her. A moment's frozen panic. Then she spun around and tried to run, butting a stranger hard. He looked at her curiously—

"Gomen, gomen," she apologized hastily.

Her mind whirled—Hawaii, the island of glass beaches, where the insistent Japanese-American and the mute child—Yoshiro Nakamura, the one who called himself "Josh"—on the glass beach under the stars—emotions shattering like old crystal—

"I thought," he said slowly, "that you must have committed suicide, wasn't that the gist of the story. . . ?"

"No! It was a myth! The black samurai—"

"Ryoko Ishida!" he blurted out. The crowd parted instantly, staring, faces shocked with recognition. The samurai moved threateningly, faces gleaming, then

Earthquake!

"Oh, Christ!" Nakamura said in English. He seized her. He pushed at the crowd. They broke free of the huddle as the fountain cracked open.

"Quick! Into the museum, under the doorway! It's the safest place!" she whispered.

What was the man doing here? She felt the question buzzing, like an annoying insect, in her mind. He grabbed her hand and they raced for the building that was already trembling like a dragon waking to darkness.

Her face was buried in his cloak. Everything was completely black, but the screaming shrilled through the thick darkness—

"Can't you go any faster?" he said, savagely gripping her arm. The doorway could not be more than 200 meters away, but the crowd swelled around them, pushing them back. She smelled the dirty cloth in her face, tasted the caked sweat, as she stumbled through the tidewall. And they found the steps, and the three of them clambered up them.

She felt warm blood on her fingers, her own, from a jagged stone that had gone clattering down the steps behind them. There was the doorway, she saw as the cloak fell from her face.

She pushed an old man out of the way in her haste. They stood under the doorway; it was heavy with baroque, pseudo-European reliefs in the stone. With a clang the doors had ripped and rattled down the steps, crushing the old man. She stifled a cry, then, and moved closer to her new friend. The broken moonlight illuminated part of the step in front of them; everything else was dark, a dense darkness from which the screaming came as a single note sustained by a *Gagaku* orchestra, penetrating the percussion of tumbling rocks . . .

They squeezed the boy between them. (There was something wrong with that boy, she remembered. What had it been?)

"Are they gone, the black samurai?" she whispered.

He was staring abstractedly, dead-eyed, into the walling emptiness.

"Are they gone. . . ?" she said again. This time she shouted; another tremor had begun.

"I think so . . ."

The doorway still held, but behind her walls were ripping like curtains. "Why are they pursuing you?" he asked her above the thundering.

"I'm with the Ishida project, of course!" Then she added, "Of course you've never heard of it. They're supposed to kill us all . . ." were they safe now? She walled her mind in from the continuous wailing.

"The Ishida project? That's what I came here to find . . . *duck!*" She did, quickly.

"So . . . you were the second person to break into Toda's house. We missed each other by only a few minutes." He broke away from her and stared, then.

She laughed out loud; so did he. But the boy was silent. It was so surprising that there seemed to be no comment she could make, so she just said: "I am glad the museum has been broken open by this earthquake; there are some objects I would like to see, before the ships leave for the stars . . . you know the museum was closed by the Ministry of Ending."

"It's true? I can still volunteer? It isn't just some fantasy of people without hope, then?"

"Of course it's true." But she remembered her father, then, and just listened to the rhythm of the rocks falling, steadily.

"Do you often have earthquakes, then?" He wouldn't leave her alone to think.

"Yes. No. This one is just a little one, really, compared to some we've had." She thought suddenly of the films she had seen, the great 'Quake of '89 . . . *child, oh child, you are mayflies that fizzle in the sunlight* . . . she remembered the whale, then, vividly as a recurring dream.

"Christ," he said suddenly.

They were silent, thinking their own thoughts. The roar went on and on.

"What are you doing in Japan?" She had to shout.

"Running away!"

"From what?"

"Not *from . . . to!*"

She closed her eyes, then, thinking of the island, thrown up by a volcano, terribly vulnerable, with the tall needles gleaming in the moons' light. I suppose I will never visit my father's tomb, now, she thought. I will take this man with me, to Nathan and to the others. He's a link between their kind and mine. A permanent alien. Like me.

Then she thought: how could I have disregarded him, when I met him in Hawaii? What kind of a man is he, to have crossed half the dead world, rejecting his whole life, to come here? As I have, she thought then. We're the same, somehow.

But she rejected her analogy immediately, as somehow too contrived, too perfect; for these happenings were no work of art, no haiku where everything is in balance.

"How did you hear of the Ishida project?"

"Through the Abbot I stayed with, at the Golden Pagoda in Kyoto. It nearly killed him to tell me, the shame of it . . ."

Half to herself, she said: "There *are* patterns, then."

"What do you mean?"

"The predecessor of the Abbot made a prophecy once. Everyone thought he was mad, but . . . he foretold how my father and Takahashi would become implacable enemies. It didn't really happen that way; my father is dead."

"Takahashi, too."

"So they say."

And the roar went on. Somehow, she felt quite free from fear. Even while a hail of death crashed about them. She moved closer to him, conscious of some vague, preconscious emotion—

"Didi," Josh said quietly.

Without a sound the boy slipped quickly aside, remaining part of them but outside, and the two of them collapsed into a shattering embrace.

The intimacy of it disturbed her profoundly. This is all

wrong! she thought. Nothing has been arranged, we haven't been introduced by our parents, it's all improper. Her body shuddered with pleasure and guilt, and with the sensuous warmth.

For a few seconds they were three-in-one—somehow the boy was never out of the picture.

This doesn't feel as wrong as it should, she thought. But why?

Then she remembered why. It was the end of the world. And the roar went on.

I'm imagining this, Josh thought.

Aftermath of earthquake, a stillness shot through with light-arrows through crack-riddled ceilings onto broken stone steps, a girl from a year-old memory, but changed, in command of him.

"Quick." She slipped away, moisture from her hand still clinging to his fingers. Didi, their shadow, shadowed. *What's happening to me?* he thought.

He rejected the idea of love.

He looked at the ruined fountain beside which the body of Utaemon the actor lay, small, crushed, his powder-white face translated from the face of Ryoko and transfigured by the faintest of smiles. Ryoko was talking now, telling him the truths of which he had only heard distorted rumors.

"There's no more time now. I have to take you to Sapporo, as quickly as possible; you'll be the last person we can take I suppose. There was so much I was going to do here, so many unfinished strands of the story I was to have tied up! . . . to visit my father's grave, to find out what *really* is going on here, to see *fujisan*. That, at least, we can do . . ."

They walked down corridors, some roofless, past chained-up doorways that the quake had cracked, past ground windows boarded up or shattered or standing in between nonexistent walls. "Come on," said Ryoko impatiently. She took his hand again, and they both became excited by each other's closeness and had to stand still together for a moment, while the boy stood half-mocking them.

A light snow of petals carpeted the rich carpets. "Look," said Ryoko. "In the light, through the roof-chinks, the petals aren't pink any more. They're a strange off-white. It's the colors of the night."

Josh did not really understand, so he squeezed her hand gently. She said, "Cherry petals are very sad; they are warriors who have died young." (And even Josh knew this; it was an old Japanese metaphor, that had sometimes come to the lips of *obasan* in a land with no cherry blossoms . . .)

The corridors forked, and forked again.

Ming bowls had slid into a heap on one end of a long glass case, blue and white and fragmented into shards peppered with shiny glass-pieces, dull red of pulverized stoneware dusting the floor, and

"Before I told my father about the whale, we came here," Ryoko was saying. "We looked at the old teabowl and cried our hearts out."

Josh said, "I had a teabowl once."

Didi shadowed. They all huddled closer together. Josh felt a chill, as the spring wind rose and tore through the violated walls and touched the centuries of dead art for the first time.

An Egyptian sarcophagus had spilled its contents into the floor, the mummy splintered in two pieces, and broken alabaster jars, and an Indian deva with a hundred hands over the mummy in a necrophilic embrace, and

"This room, here," said Ryoko. Josh saw her, how she trembled. The brothers followed her . . . the roof was intact here, so it was dark.

"Yes, we'll hide until we can take the bullet train," Ryoko was saying at the doorway, "you don't have to pay anymore, then a boat to the island. We have friends in the North, people we can trust. You're the last one, you know. Soon—"

Josh thought of the journey. He could see nothing. It seemed to come to an end with the needles, silvery-straight, piercing the night; beyond that he could imagine nothing . . . the stars were nothing to him, not a romantic longing, not a new page in the history of man; they were only something towards which he was running, blindly, something that symbolized the end of his dissatisfaction. But now the pattern made sense. He was content to take on faith the proposition that, to leave his unhappiness behind, he must leave behind the whole world.

"What are you thinking of?" Ryoko said.

"Silver needles gleaming in the night," he said. And

with those words they kissed, for the first time. "And you?"

"My father," said Ryoko. They kissed again.

"This isn't love," said Josh. "It's something in the way we've been thrown together, something illogical."

"It doesn't matter anymore," said Ryoko. "Now I really understand. The world is ending." And they kissed a third time, and stepped into the little darkness.

"Light?" said Ryoko. "It's so dark, we'll have to get used to it first."

In the middle of the room, a glass case. The three of them, hands linked, went to it, and waited.

"I don't see anything," said Josh. Was the light tricking him? Would they have to wait a while longer, to see more clearly?

"A few more seconds. It's a dark object . . ."

They waited. Ryoko said, "It's not there!"

Josh felt her hand shaking, and knew how desolated she was, and wished he could understand this Japanese fascination with twisted objects. She didn't make a sound but he knew she was crying.

Didi uttered a little moan, and Josh looked up . . . into an empty face.

"It's over, you idle dreamers!" A muffled, metal voice. The three moved closer together.

In the shadows black samurai moved, Josh couldn't tell how many. Suddenly the air was thick with their breathing.

Leather hands pried the three apart. Rope bit into him, jerking him backwards. "What are you doing to us?"

No answer. Only the swift rustling of the black garments, the shifting of mirror-faces.

"Let us go! We aren't doing anything wrong . . ." he screamed at the empty face. A hideous laughter filled the room.

"You're from *Takahashi!*" Ryoko grated.

They didn't answer. They were all trussed-up now, like chickens for the oven. Josh couldn't move a muscle. He felt the rag being shoved into his mouth and tied. Pain dug into the back of his neck. He tried to talk but it hurt too much. Ryoko whimpered softly somewhere. And darkness, thick darkness.

"You can't escape." The voice, implacable and dispassionate. "You can't destroy the majesty of this final vision, you know. You can't pollute the purity of the Ending."

They're going to kill us!

"Think we're barbarians, don't you? Think we're going to kill you, don't you? The Death Lord does not kill, he only helps people to kill themselves. Why have you people listened to the puny clamorings of immigrants, to the un-Japanese whinings of the heretic Ishida? Come! Come! You are going to Shikoku."

They were pushed out of the room. All along the corridor, rows of black-garbed warriors, tall and straight and inhumanly still, waiting.

"Move, you three! Still afraid of being killed, aren't you? Well, it's mercy we are going to give you! Come, come!"

The boot smashed into the base of his spine. Pain fireworked all over him. He lurched forward—

An alien music, tragedy-tinged, a high keening transsected the darkness, the wind weaving a passionate counterpoint around it, and the night-paled petals raining over them, and

A small voice—Ryoko's—from behind a gag, through curtains of pain—"Whale song! Whale song!"

How? How? Pain pounding him as he stumbled forward, the high song tingling through the night air, where was it coming from? where? Stumbling now, falling, roused by another kick, lost, going from darkness to darkness, and then divining, suddenly, the source of the music, the face beside him, eyes closed, boyish form frozen by terror, the air resounding, humming,

Didi.

Part Three

SUMMER GRASSES

natsu-gusa ya
tsuwamono-domo ga
yume no ato

(only summer grasses,
after the mighty warriors,
after their dreams of glory)

—Basho (1644–1694)

Chapter 18

SUMMER, 2024

Ryoko saw a silver faceless face gleaming in the blackness. Embrace your destiny, *it said.* Drink the poison. . . .

The sea surged, a whale leapt over the moon which was no longer in pieces. . . .

"No!" She awoke to blackness.

Groping, she found the wall. She found the edge of her pallet, a flimsy thing of stuffed cotton on a floor that smelled of new *tatami.*

The wall.

She skimmed her fingers along it. Slime oozed. There was a small grille, about 25 centimeters long; a hot wind stroked at her fingers. So it was night, then: by day she would be able to see.

But for now there was a darkness almost unnaturally intense, and there were no stars, no moons. Cloud must be shrouding the sky.

Where am I? How long have I been here?

She could not tell. She remembered only the ride, parts of it; a black carriage, drawn by sickly black horses, being trussed up, being injected with some sedative or another, blackness—

And then she was conscious of a whispering in the room.

It was almost beneath the threshold of audibility. It was a comforting voice such as her mother might have used when she was child, a little sensual, very soft and warm. . . .

And why did the Death Lord not have you killed? You should be grateful for that, said the voice. *You should be grateful to him who opens the door into Beauty for you. Here we do not kill. We merely open doors, so that when the beautiful moment comes you will give yourself freely into that state of being. . . .*

It was perhaps a *Noh* actor's voice, Ryoko thought, getting drowsier . . . but there was nothing else to listen to, and the voice continued, melting her down, persuading her . . . she was sinking through beds of cloud into soft warm darkness. . . .

RYOKO! DON'T FALL IN!

The death scream of a very small child.

"Who's that?" Ryoko called out. It wasn't her own voice, it wasn't the droning, persuasive voice, it wasn't any part of her—

RYOKO!

And she slid into full wakefulness.

"Who's there?" she said again.

"What do you mean?" she heard Josh's voice; he, too, seemed to have been asleep. "Where are we?" Ryoko strained her eyes, but the darkness was almost total. "Where are you?" she heard Josh say. It was muffled, and not just from drowsiness, she thought.

"Are you in this room?" she said. She ran her fingers along the wall until she reached a corner, then crept along the wall, hugging the slime, until she ascertained that the wall was featureless except for that one grille and another, wider one that seemed to lead into a corridor, something she couldn't see. Josh must be in a cell like hers, then, in the next one perhaps. "Tap your wall," she said.

Tap-tap-tap . . . she followed the sound. It was the wall opposite the grille with the wind from outside. Putting her ear there, she spoke again. "Josh?"

"Do you know where we are?" came the muffled sound.

Ryoko shivered, although the room was warm, too warm in fact. "This is Shikoku, I think," she said. . . .

"Shikoku? The rice district?"

"I forgot," Ryoko said, "you can't write Japanese . . . this is the same name, but the character *shi* has been replaced by another character, *shi*, for death . . . this is the Death Land that Takahashi's 'ghost' always mentioned . . . this is where people come to die, Josh."

"They'll kill us?"

"I don't know."

RYOKO!

"Who was that?" she cried, startled.

"What?" came Josh's voice.

Ryoko, this is Didi, came a voice in her mind. *Josh can't hear me. I can talk to you in my head, because you're a little bit like* them. *One of* them *once talked to you.*

"Ryoko, Ryoko . . ." said Josh.

"Josh, be quiet a moment, I'm hearing something very strange." Then she said . . . "You're the child that goes around with Yoshiro, the one who never talks, the one there's something wrong with?"

Yes. Yes.

Her mind burst with the image of the leaping whale, transsecting a starlit sky across the silhouette of a silver-treed island in the gray sea . . . "Josh!" she called. "Do you remember this picture of the whale and the island?" And she thought the picture, as hard as she could.

Silver trees, the leaping whale . . . "Yes, yes . . . what's going on?" came Josh's strange, strangled voice. . . .

Ryoko was trembling. Hard.

Ryoko, whatever you do, don't listen to the background voices! They're trying to hypnotize you, to brainwash you into suicide! . . . this is a terrible, terrible place; I've sent my mind out and heard other minds, lost minds, dead minds. The person who rules here—

Ryoko nodded. "Ryoko!" came Josh's voice again.

"Wait, I'm listening to this other voice—"

Ryoko, Yoshiro can't hear me. I can't get through to him. But I'm blocking the sounds in his cell. He's weaker than we are, Ryoko. You can hear whales talk, you can understand a little of their nature, but I'm on the inside, trapped in this body . . . I'm a complete throwback, in some ways! I can see the dance of atoms, the ballet of energy-particles! Perceiving is controlling . . . I've been working on controlling, Ryoko. But I have to work more.

And it's making me so weak . . . Ryoko felt the edge of a terrible sadness. Then the presence left her.

She felt warm all over, comforted.

But the voices started to slip into her consciousness again, telling her about death, how beautiful death was, how much she needed to die. She knew that Didi had to protect Josh more than her, and that she should be able to resist. But it was almost like the time when she had almost thrown herself from the boat, that day a year ago, on the journey to Aishima.

Compassion is stronger than honor! she told herself.

But the voice whispered: *Adherence to honor is the most beautiful of virtues. We are honor-bound to make the Ending of the world the most beautiful of possible endings . . . for the meaning of a haiku is truly illuminated only in its last line.*

"Josh!" she called.

"Yes?"

"Whatever you do, don't let them persuade you to kill yourself. They want us to kill ourselves; they don't want us ever to leave the planet; it ruins the whole thing if a single person escapes."

"What do you mean?" said Josh. "Hundreds of people are leaving, aren't they? Isn't the Ishida project full of volunteers?"

"You and I are the only Japanese. The pursuit of beauty is irrelevant, Josh, to the others. Whoever is in control here does not really consider the others in his perfect vision of ending . . ."

"But I'm American!" Josh said, anguished.

"No," said Ryoko, tired, stern. *We are the children of the whale. It must show through, somehow; culture isn't that deep, it's only an overlay . . .*

There was light now. Just a little. She turned to see the grille glow reddish. She called Josh's name but there was no answer; perhaps he was at his window too. She clambered over and stood on tiptoe, her eyes just making it to the opening.

The false Mount Fuji that she had seen from the train station a long time before dominated the horizon. In the foreground was a roller coaster, a merry-go-round, a ferris-wheel, tents . . . new-looking, shiny. Just at her eye-level, a conveyor belt moved.

She started back. A corpse glared at her. It was a plague-corpse, green and twisted. She retched, the corpse rolled onward . . . when she turned her head she saw a mound of corpses moving in from the right. The belt was badly oiled and was squeaking. . . .

Ryoko let out a gasp as a corpse slithered by.

It wasn't a corpse! The greenish, withered body was breathing still. The face was close to Ryoko's face; she could have felt its breath. An almost sweet odor clung to the body. It was a face of resignation, of total despair, not human really.

"Can you talk?" Ryoko said.

But the body rolled past her, and the conveyor belt squeaked inexorably on its way.

She heard Josh tapping on the wall, and ran to it.

"They're going to kill us!" he rasped in English.

And Ryoko said: "No, I don't think so." But she was no longer hopeful.

The voice came softly to her, whispering of beauty and duty. "I don't hear you, I don't hear you!" she said, hysterical. She tried to hold back the tears that were on the verge of gushing out, and then abandoned herself to them, thinking *I'll get it over with at least.*

Josh was banging wildly. "What's happening, why are you making all that noise?" he was saying. "Are they doing something to you?" She wanted him beside her, she wanted him to touch her, to comfort her, even though she knew he could be no real comfort . . .

DIDI! she cried out with her mind.

And at once a presence reassured her, as though a whale had come forth out of the deep.

She waited for what would happen next.

Chapter 19

The circle is closing. The thing of beauty is taking shape.

"Let the cricket live," he mused aloud; and he unclenched his fist and allowed the creature to limp along the *tatami.* Its hind legs gathered strength as it reached the grooves where the *shoji* had been pushed wide open to the summer; soon it was hopping again, blithely unaware of its brush with death.

With the Death Lord himself.

Who smiled softly, full of compassion for the cricket. And envy for it, too; for the world belonged to them now, to these creatures of primal innocence, and not to the creatures of intelligence and shame. *I am grateful for consciousness,* he thought, *for I can perceive beauty, and I can shape beauty. . . .*

Idly he patted the cushion he was sitting on, picked up the bowl of green tea that a Deathbound had just served him, drank deeply, savoring its taste; and turned to face Kawaguchi.

Kawaguchi was a fool. The Death Lord selected his most authoritative voice, addressing him sternly, like a menial: "They are here?"

"Yes, Death Lord. They are in individual cells; they

have been saturated with the continuous tape recordings for some time now," said Kawaguchi. Death Lord motioned for him to take tea; when he saw that there was no teabowl on the table except for *that one,* he called for another. . . .

"Kawaguchi, do you think it wrong that I have removed *this* from Ueno, for my own use? Is this clinging to worldly things?"

"I have no idea."

Takahashi turned away. His eyes lingered on the teabowl—not the ones they were drinking from, but *the* teabowl, now sitting in the middle of the table.

Twisted and lovely. *Fujisan.*

When the three have agreed to die, there's an end of it.

"Shall I give you the statistics, Lord?"

"No need! They are all doomed anyway," Takahashi said harshly. "Whether it takes a year or more or less is immaterial. For the plan centers on those three alone!"

"Sir, the population of Japan is presently 85 percent immigrant. Plague-death has accounted for a goodly percentage of our deaths, but self-immolation is slightly more significant statistically . . . Shikoku now processes several thousand voluntary deaths per day."

"I know it's working effectively! But what about those three, the man and the boy and the girl?"

"You could always—"

"I know what you are saying!" Takahashi grated. "You compromiser! You would have me *murder* those three people, just to repair a tiny flaw in my perfect image of Ending? That murder would be a bigger flaw than anything we could perpetrate otherwise. Remember, Shikoku is a land of compassion, of honor, of rectitude! We give beauty here, not criminality!" Takahashi was trembling with rage.

Am I cheating? The thought brushed against his mind, insistent.

Ha! How can I cheat? he answered himself, *when I myself am the artist?*

"These are your final instructions, Kawaguchi. You are to show our three guests the true meaning of their existence. You shall release them from their cells, reason with them, make them accept their destiny with grace. They're *Japanese* people! They *must* understand!"

(Do they really understand? he found himself thinking. *Those lost souls who come here, herded by train-*

loads, do they see the beauty as I see it? Or are they just obeying the group instinct?)

Kawaguchi bowed.

Takahashi watched the teabowl *fujisan,* the way it almost grew out of the wood of the table, a four-dimensional organism quick-frozen in time . . . and listened to the crickets and the frogs. He took more tea.

Deliberately, he said: "And, Kawaguchi, when those three people have been liberated from their self-delusions, I will liberate you too. You will be able to join your ancestors. Think of that."

Kawaguchi bowed several times, thanking him profusely.

"No need to thank me," said Takahashi magnanimously. And he allowed himself a compassionate smile.

I free you, just as I freed that harmless little cricket, he thought, and I smile the same smile. *How beautiful these last days are, how beautiful the last line of the haiku.*

But he retracted the smile, knowing he must not be soft or he would lose face. "Go now!" he said abruptly. "Fulfill your purpose, so that you may salute your sword and enter the world of truth!"

Takahashi watched Kawaguchi's back as he bowed and departed. And sat in thought for some long moments.

Am I cheating? came the thought, more persistent.

Takahashi rose and walked into the garden. The broken moons had already risen, before the sunset; and the chirpings never ceased. He strode back and forth for about ten minutes; then he summoned one of the Deathbound, a woman in a white kimono, and told her to bring him his sword from the audience chamber. Presently she brought it, laid it on the table beside the teabowl, took away the tea-things, and departed, in quick, noiseless movements. Takahashi sat and stared at the two things, the sword and the teabowl, for a very long time.

Suppose I am cheating.

I am not cheating!

Then why do I not experience satori?

At last. He had dared to admit it to himself. Despite his constant preoccupation with death and beauty, he had experienced no moment of transcendent enlightenment. No *satori.*

He doubted.

Quick! Take the sword, end the doubt! Plunge it

through your entrails right now, don't wait for doubt to destroy you . . . content yourself, the ending is inevitable now!

But he was still attached to material things: for he needed to see for himself the end of the haiku. . . .

His hand was on the sword.

Now!

But Takahashi knew that he would wait until the very end. At least until the three renegades were inescapably woven into the great plan. He was too close to perfection to give up now.

He toyed with the teabowl, turning it slowly in the light. Its strained beauty made him ache inside. . . .

Enigmas within enigmas.

The three stumbled into the light. Josh blinked, struggled uselessly against the arms of the two black samurai who had him pinioned.

"Release them," came a voice, nasal, soft. An oldish man faced them, dressed so elaborately that his features were lost in the mass of robes. . . .

"Kawaguchi!" he heard Ryoko say.

The old man looked at them without seeming to see them. "The three of you . . . we are transferring you to decent quarters, as befits the most honored guests of the Death Lord. But first, a tour of the facilities: as you will see, we have many such facilities, all designed for maximum convenience when you choose to select your moment of truth. Now—answer me!" His voice was sharp, suddenly.

"Hai," said Ryoko.

"Hai," said Josh, and turned to his brother. *Why do I put you through this, Didi, when you're so totally innocent?*

Didi said nothing. "Why does he not speak?" demanded Kawaguchi.

Josh said, "It's not his fault. He was born that way."

"I see. Then—since he is not fully in control of his senses anyway—it may not be necessary to wait for him to exercise his option of self-extinction," Kawaguchi said, slyly.

"No!" Josh said, struggling to reach his brother, who only stared serenely ahead, expressionless.

"Come, the grand tour," said Kawaguchi, and the three were released. For the rest of the day the guards folowed them, each silver-faced and indistinguishable, and did not lay hands on them. But Josh felt as captive as ever.

Is this what I ran away for? he thought, bitter.

His eyes were used to the light now. He saw that they were standing outside, on a pathway. In the background loomed a mountain—Mount Fuji, it looked like, from the pictures he had seen and from *obasan*'s descriptions —but it flickered . . . not exactly flickered, but there were moments when it seemed transparent, an illusion of a mountain.

At the foot of the mountain was a great lake, and from the path where he stood up to the lake a profusion of wild grasses, growing without order or arrangement . . . and a gigantic roller coaster, and a half-dozen or so low pavilions, newly-built.

He turned around and saw more buildings, and a wall that seemed to run as far as he could see in either direction.

"This is Shikoku, the Death Land," said Kawaguchi smiling. "This is where those who have chosen the way to beauty can spend their final days, amid beautiful things, until the time comes for them . . . but first you must put on the garments of the Deathbound."

They were led into a small hut, where a black samurai issued them with shapeless white *kimono* and waited, watching, while they donned them. Then they were led outside again. It was early morning, and the sun behind Mount Fuji seemed to shine right through the mountain, giving it an unearthly glow.

"Now follow us," said Kawaguchi. They walked across the grass to the lake-shore, and then Josh saw that there was a boat waiting for them, so they stepped on and the black samurai rowed, and they were squeezed together on wet planks, he between Ryoko and Didi, Kawaguchi facing them, smiling the whole time, an ingratiating, poisonous smile.

Presently they came to the foot of a mountain. It was not Mount Fuji; that had disappeared. It was only a little hill, actually, that cliffed out over the lake; there was an escalator to the top, and an unending stream of people, pouring out of buses, all in identical white *kimono,* waiting patiently in line, ascending one by one . . .

"This is one of our most popular facilities," said Kawaguchi. They had left the boat and were walking towards the escalator.

The faces of the people! Josh was strangely moved. They were in tears, some of them, but most had frozen, dispassionate expressions. There were lovers, holding hands. There were old men, children. They stood at the base of the escalator, watching the faces glide past.

"What are they doing?" said Josh.

"You ignorant fool! How can you ask?" said Kawaguchi. He turned abruptly and motioned them to follow. Hidden from the escalator's viewpoint by an outcropping of the rock was an elevator. Kawaguchi pressed the button; the door opened instantly, and he and the three stepped in. Two of the faceless ones followed.

They reached a little hut on the top of the hill, and followed Kawaguchi to the cliff-edge. About ten meters away from them, an old man was preparing to jump off the cliff.

Josh watched . . . he stripped off his clothes, this old man, and his body was pitifully emaciated. There were plague-signs on him; the skin was a little green. The man stood in thought for a while, then took a little run and jumped.

Next was a vigorous young man who jumped with a yell of *banzai!*

Next was a woman who cried the whole time.

Next—

"Is this going to happen to us?" Josh said to Kawaguchi. "Are you going to force all of us to commit suicide?"

Kawaguchi smiled again. "We are not murderers, Nakamura," he said. "We are merely architects of a beautiful dream."

Two old people, a man and a woman, jumped, hands linked, over the edge. Josh could not take his eyes off that ledge. They had a serenity that. . . .

He realized suddenly that he longed for such a peace himself.

No! cried a faint voice inside him. He turned around and looked at his little brother, who seemed to be in a trance. . . .

Kawaguchi went on, "After a time you will come to see the beauty of this picture. At that time you yourself will select self-destruction rather than face the shame of blighting the perfection of Ending . . . it *is* beautiful, is it not?"

Josh was confused. "No," he said quickly, "it's murder!"

"It is beautiful!" The smile was fixed on now.

The two samurai moved towards him, hands on scabbards . . .

"Yes," said Josh, sighing heavily. And perhaps it was. And perhaps it was . . . a little girl jumped over the edge, singing to herself. . . .

My whole life I've been running, thought Josh. *First from the bombs, then from Hawaii, then. . . . Maybe this is the only possible escape!*

No, Josh! cried the little voice again, and again his eye was drawn to his brother, standing eyes closed, huddled close to Ryoko. *Oh Christ,* he said to the voice, *for Christ's sake protect me from this, I think I really want to do it—*

"Shall we move on?" said Kawaguchi.

Where had Mount Fuji gone to? On the boat ride, all the time, it dominated the horizon, glowing in the morning light. . . .

He was about to ask Kawaguchi, but Ryoko interposed: "The mountain, Mount Fuji I mean, not this hillock we're standing on . . . it's nowhere near here, is it? It's holographic. Before the Millennial War people created such wonders routinely, didn't they? So where are we, really?"

"What is reality?" said Kawaguchi.

Reluctantly Josh turned away from the sight of the suiciders and they took the elevator again. The lines were no shorter at the base of the escalator; more buses were waiting, more buses were unloading. In the parking lot a black electric Toyota was awaiting them.

Josh heard Ryoko gasp when she saw it.

"The chauffeur . . . my father's old chauffeur, the American!" she whispered to Josh.

He was the first caucasian Josh had seen since their arrival in Shikoku . . . why was he serving the Death People? Why wasn't he running off to join the Ishida project?

Kawaguchi got in in front and indicated that they should sit in the back. They squeezed in, with Didi between them, and the black samurai flanking them on either side.

"John," Ryoko said. . . .

The driver turned around. "You're supposed to be dead!" he said. "I saw the play . . ." Kawaguchi commanded silence with a look.

"There is a place even for non-Japanese," he said, "in helping us achieve our ends . . ." The car began to move.

Looking ahead, Josh saw that Mount Fuji had reappeared.

Can't I just get it over with, give in . . . ?

The car drove through well-paved roads, something Josh had never seen since his childhood, past almost too-perfect rice-fields. It was coming up to noon, and Josh was getting hungrier.

Now and then they would see lines of people in white robes, waiting for something; streaming out of buses, just walking, with the silver-faced samurai guarding them . . . the Death Lord's realm was vast, then. Who was this Death Lord? He must be a madman, to want to force everyone to die like this, and yet—they were doing it. It was wrong, though, wrong!

But the suiciders had seemed so happy; happier than Josh had ever felt. They seemed secure. Was this how one made one's peace with the world, was this the only escape?

The car sped along, encountering no others. They reached a clump of houses and pavilions, over which ran a roller coaster, twisting in and out of the buildings, soaring up—

Josh followed the mazelike lines of the roller coaster, and suddenly saw—

At the end, at the bottom of a high hill, the coaster was broken off. There was a drop onto cement, perhaps 80 feet. It was another suicide device!

They got out of the car. Josh saw that a coaster car, full of white-robed people, was grinding up one of the hills . . . he knew what was going to happen.

"Open your eyes!" Kawaguchi said, and he felt the arms of the black samurai on him. He did so. A shriek of utter terror rent the air. He looked up. The coaster had dropped the first hill and was rounding a curve. The screaming went on and on—

"Listen to the sounds of joy," said Kawaguchi. "Is it not like the sounds made by whales, as they contemplate utter beauty in the darkness of the sea?"

Josh saw Ryoko start. Something had struck home.

He saw what was happening now. Sickness hit him. The

coaster reached the last hill and derailed, spilling its cargo. The screaming was chaotic—

There was a giant thud. Then silence.

"It is rather well designed, I think; the original came from Fuji Highland, an amusement park in the foothills of Mount Fuji in the twentieth century. The cars all come apart very easily and can as easily be reassembled. It's for the adventurous, or for those who feel their shame needs a special kind of expiation."

Josh wanted to run forward and look—he had to see—

"Restrain him!" came Kawaguchi's voice.

The arms pinned him again. He saw Ryoko lift her hands to cover up Didi's eyes. *Why did I bring him at all? He understands nothing, he's just a victim. . . .*

Kawaguchi looked at them with his smug smile, and Josh stared at the patterns on his robe, gold filigree stitched onto purple and red cloth . . . "But there is more," Kawaguchi said. "Come . . ."

After another drive they reached a walled enclosure. It was of gray brick and was some twenty feet high. A black guard saluted and allowed them to enter through rust-reddened iron gates.

They passed through another door and Josh perceived that they were enclosed completely in glass, and that the temperature had dropped. The glass roof was ribbed with metallic ribbons.

It was a cherry grove . . . in perpetual spring. An artificial wind blew through the place, whirling the clouds of cherry blossoms—

"We use accelerated growth patterns on the nurslings, and transfer the cherry trees here whenever necessary, uprooting the old ones . . . this is our garden of contemplation, where those of the black samurai who are ready may take the way to beauty."

It was crazier and crazier! There were far too many petals, the spring was obviously an unnatural one, the petals were flying about in the most artificial spring tempest, the scent was intense and overpowering . . . they had walked down a carefully graveled path for only a few minutes when Josh stopped to stare.

Under a cherry tree, one of the black samurai sat, his black vestments open to the waist. He had disemboweled himself. He was still alive; he stared back at Josh, and Josh could see that the man was clenching back agony, was straining to keep his meditative position—

"They are noble, aren't they," Kawaguchi said, "our black samurai, guardians of the plan."

Those eyes! Was this the great ecstacy that he had been told about?

Ryoko bent over the man and said, quietly, "Are you in pain?"

The man nodded. . . .

Josh knelt down and stared at the man's face as though he were not there. Then he said, "Is this what you wanted? Is this your perfect Ending, is this all true?" For a moment he wished that the man would say yes. He wished that *something* would be true!

"Please," he said, "tell me how beautiful it is . . ."

But the man was dead. Josh felt betrayed, illogically. The man was empty now. Had he experienced the thing they called *satori?* Slowly Josh got up.

Kawaguchi studied him, then said, "You were moved, weren't you?"

"Yes." It was a whisper.

"Come."

They walked further in the cherry grove, the pink-snowed wind playing with their faces. Others of the black samurai were sitting in meditation under the cherry trees: some contemplating their daggers, some with their arms upraised, ready to strike, others merely sitting and thinking in puddles of silence, others dead.

They went on with the tour, driving through more fields, viewing more scenes of death. . . .

And finally they came to a theater. It was open air, under the streaming afternoon sunlight, and they were playing *The Romance of the Young Girl and the Whale.* White-robed, the Deathbound sat on the ground, rapt. . . .

Josh recognized the players. "But those people are dead!" he blurted out.

Ryoko touched his hand. "Holographic theater, Josh. All the old technology . . ." And Josh suddenly remembered the room at the Hilo Hilton, where Joey the preek sat making his crazy prophecies and the machines hummed and the models of people danced and surfed and moved about.

The play proceeded, just as he remembered it in Ueno park. It was the dance of first contact, when Ryoko had met the whale. The dead Utaemon moved with feline grace across the flagstones which ended abruptly and became summer grasses. . . .

Kawaguchi was silent for a long time. Josh saw how Ryoko was absorbed by the play; he wondered which she thought more beautiful, the real life she had led or the life they had created for her in the play . . . and after the beautiful suicide scene, the play ended. Most of the Deathbound wandered away, and the flagstoned open-air stage dissolved into more grass.

They had a voice, from hidden loudspeakers. Josh and Ryoko were frozen for a moment. It was Ryoko's voice.

". . . when they danced, they were like Buddhas. They were full of compassion. Their lives had become pure music; they slapped their bodies joyously on the water, collapsing from exhaustion. They were enlightened, they had loosed completely the bonds with material things—

"Whales perceive very finely. They see the dance of subatomic particles, I think, that's how they alter reality, controlling by perceiving, at least that's how I felt, trapped by the whale's mind . . . How they danced! How they danced the dance of death, forgetting everything, becoming one with the ultimate truth. . . ." It was a steady voice. A voice full of confidence, full of joy.

Josh had never heard Ryoko speak with that voice before, except perhaps when she had talked to them in Hawaii, before he really knew her. It was a self he could not really understand.

"It isn't true anymore!" Ryoko cried. "I was younger, I was overwhelmed. How could you use what I said in the past to turn people to death! How could you! We're people, too, no matter what our distant ancestry; we've interbred with humans . . . you have no right to do this!"

Josh took her in his arms, then, and they both wept, and Didi stood just outside the circle of those too, watching.

"Come on," Kawaguchi said abruptly. They were in the car again, and this time Josh recognized that they were coming close to the cells where they had been imprisoned at first. They drove along a giant wall that dominated everything, and beyond the first group of structures Josh saw the things he had first seen that day: the lake, the Mount Fuji that he knew now to be an illusion, the distant roller coaster.

How long before I give up running away and line up and jump or stuff a dagger in my guts?

They got out of the car in front of a large circular building. "One more thing," Kawaguchi said, "before I free you to eat and sleep."

They entered the building.

It was a giant ballroom. A *gagaku* ensemble played shrilly on a platform in the middle, the reed instruments shrieking, the drums crashing. It was an ugly sound, Josh thought; a scary sound too.

All over the floor were dancers. Their faces were calm, but their bodies thrashed around in wild movements, out of time with the music. They leapt and cartwheeled, some of them, while others moved slowly, jerkily. Their white *kimono* were torn, some of them had shed their clothes and were reeling about the room.

"Our own deathdance," Kawaguchi said above the din.

"It's grotesque!" said Ryoko. "It's nothing like the way it should be!"

"We are but humans, are we not?" Kawaguchi shouted. "We ape our divine ancestors in what ways we can!"

The *gagaku* music crescendoed in earsplitting clusters of dissonances—

Josh walked out among the dancers. The weird and alien screechings assaulted his ears. Drums and bells crashed. He did not think that this was real *gagaku* music; it was a crazy, orderless improvisation, frenzied and unmusical. He saw the faces of the musicians, wildly contorted as they pounded on the *gagaku* drums, twisted as they blew into their flutes, their eyes bulging in their sweat-drenched faces. And the dancers, flailing the air and dropping, to be removed on stretchers by menials in black robes.

He turned to Ryoko, sweating. "We have to go, we have to, we have to escape this place . . ."

Kawaguchi stood in their way. "What! And not choose the rightful path?" he said. And smiled again. "But you will in the end. Reason will conquer fear. Let's leave . . ."

And they came to their quarters. It was a room in an upper floor of a building that looked out on to the place their old cells had been. It had a *tatami* floor and a little balcony, and three neat little beds in the old Japanese style, laid out on the floor with clean sheets. Kawaguchi left them. A maid (in white garments, so they knew she was really a Deathbound) served them: a meal of *tempura soba* and tea, very simple, in brown stoneware bowls; and then she left them alone.

Ryoko and Josh looked at each other for a long moment.

"What can we do now?" Josh cried out, anguished. "We're trapped! Sooner or later we'll break down!"

Ryoko turned away, looked out of the balcony once and drew the *shoji* in revulsion. "If we cannot return by the end of summer," she said, "they will go without us."

They were silent.

"What are you thinking?" said Ryoko.

"I'm thinking—I've been running a long time now, and I'm cornered, and maybe I should stop running and die."

Ryoko said, "No! There is a way, I think . . ."

In the darkness Didi sat, playing by himself. A crack in the *shoji* let the light fall beside him . . . Josh thought about his brother, about all the strange feelings he had had about him in the past.

"Do you know something about my brother?" he said.

"Only this: he isn't retarded." Josh nodded; he had always hoped . . . "He's a genetic throwback, like me in the sense that the whale first picked me to communicate with, but much more . . . it was your mother and the radiation or something . . . he is very much like the whales, Josh. He perceives the way they do. And he may be able to *change* things, the way they did . . . Josh, the whale touched me inside, he *saw* all the separate pieces of energy making me up, so he *changed* things. That is how I became impregnated. I think—if Didi tries—he could do something like that too."

"That's crazy!" said Josh. "I can hardly believe it about the whales. You can't ask me to believe . . ."

"Josh, in your cell, did you hear tapes, telling you all the reasons why you should die, whispering softly about the beauties of death?"

"No—"

"Didi stopped you from hearing them. He set up a field, blocking them from reaching you . . ."

"How do you know?"

"We communicate."

Josh's first feeling was jealousy. He loved his brother, and—"But why doesn't he talk to *me?*"

"Josh, he's telepathic! When he was born he was fully conscious! And there were a million terrified people in the room, and the bombs were dropping and the volcano was bursting and everyone knew they were going to die in the next second—and all these terrors burst in on him, in the instant of being born. Of course he won't talk! He's terrified! When he talks to me it's the faintest whisper inside my mind, and I can only hear because I once heard the whale, because I have the power of hearing . . ."

She stopped. They both heard a sound like a baby crying, very softly, to itself, a muffled sound.

"He can make sounds in the air," Ryoko whispered. "He can move the air particles. But it's very tiring for him . . ."

Josh looked at his brother. His eyes were closed again and he was sitting still, and then rocking himself back and forth on the *tatami*. And he ran to embrace the kid and comfort him, but it was like hugging a stone.

Chapter 20

Ryoko rose from the bed and went over to the *shoji.*

That night they had made love for the first time. For her at least it had been the very first. She would have demurred, but she knew that the night might be her last . . . it was a bleak and desperate lovemaking, not very comforting at all; at least it had made them tired enough to go to sleep.

Didi had played in a corner, face against the wall. She wondered if he had listened, voyeur-like, to their thoughts. He had not moved at all, but somehow she knew he had had no sleep.

She pulled the *shoji* open. Recoiled.

Bright daylight shone on the conveyor belt, which moved creakily, slowly . . . and now she could see where it led. Far to her left was the lake and the illusory Mount Fuji; and to her right, near where the towering wall stood, through a clump of trees, there curled the smoke of a bonfire. The bodies were being burned; efficiently, quickly, without any fuss. She could not see their faces from the balcony *shoji;* only the green pallor of their skin. Some were not dead. She knew what Kawaguchi had explained to her: that they were the bodies of those too weak to perform the suicide themselves, but who yet wished to contribute to Ending in a meaningful way . . . Kawaguchi had told her the statistics, too. The ethnically Japanese population was shrinking inevitably towards zero, falling to the swords of the black samurai as they raided the villages, surrendering themselves up at Shikoku. And Shikoku was expanding always.

It would eat the world—what was left of it—like a cancer.

Shuddering, she imagined herself one of the undead bodies on the conveyor belt. They were all conveyor belts: the line for the escalator to the mountain, the grotesque deathdance, the cherry grove. *This isn't how it should be!* she thought. *Each death should be a moment of supreme individuality, a moment before the dewdrop joins the ocean.*

She drew the *shoji* shut. It screeched; the grooves were not quite smooth. And let in the merest crack of light.

And watched the boy playing and the man asleep.

Then, without her being conscious of when it had begun, soft taped voices came from behind her, a revenant nightmare—

Die. Die. Die. Die.

And her own voice mixed with them all, glowing with the beauty of the whales' deathdance. . . .

And another voice: *Ryoko, you have caused all these people to die! Your voice, taped and repeated for thousands, a crucial part of their decisions to die. You are to blame! Why not face your guilt, become a part of that beauty? What can escape achieve, anyway? . . .*

Let me alone! she thought at the voices. *Let me be!* And she knew that inside she was tempted, even though she had come to a different decision, that spring night in the boat on the way to Aishima. It was so far away and there seemed no hope anymore.

"SORRY." It was Didi's voice calling from so far away. "I LOST CONCENTRATION FOR A WHILE . . . I'M SO *TIRED!*"

She hurried over to the boy. "You've been shutting them out, then, the whole time, you've been awake and screening the sounds from our minds?"

"YES! YES!"

"Why," Ryoko said, "my suffering is nothing compared to your suffering . . ." And she loved him then. The love she felt was much like the love she had felt when the whale first broke out of the dark water, so long ago. . . . She bent down and reached out to touch him, and he was like ice. His eyes were still closed; and the light from the crack in the *shoji* broke his face in half. How pathetic, she thought, and then realized that this creature that looked like a child was more powerful than she could be, and more wise, and more compassionate.

Behind the tranquillity of his face great tempests clashed. His face was like the teabowl *fujisan,* a stasis imposed over terrible conflict. She was moved by this. She wanted to embrace the boy, but was held back by her awe. So she walked over to Josh's bedding and sat down on it, looking at his face.

It was a torn face. Nothing was hidden at all.

"I love you too," she whispered; "because you're open, like a summer sky. You're much more of a child than he is . . ."

Josh opened his eyes. They smiled at each other, a trifle stupidly.

There would be another "grand tour" today. And after—

She distanced herself from her fear, hoping it would go away.

Today Kawaguchi was affable. He put on different moods like *Noh*-masks. There had been the usual disorienting ride, the usual battering with images of death. And now they were ushered in to a small room, an auditorium with perhaps a hundred seats.

The three of them sat down together; there was a little screen of the sort used to project antique movies. Ryoko remembered them from her childhood: her father had possessed one such, and they had watched old scratchy classics on the curious, flat screen, such films as *Rashomon* and *Double Suicide.* Her reverie was abruptly terminated—

Black samurai entered the room, and with jerky, efficient movements, treating the three of them like manikins, strapped them in and gripped their heads in vises so they had to face forwards and could no longer look at each other. Wires forced their eyes open.

"Didi! Josh—" she cried out, but they didn't answer. The lights began to dim very slowly . . .

"Uncomfortable, no?" came Kawaguchi's voice, jocular and mocking. "But I thought you might need a little amusement, and old movies are perhaps just the thing. Nothing we've done so far has revealed the light at the end of your tunnels of ignorance! But perhaps this little entertainment will. It is excerpted from old documentary films, taken in the twentieth century . . . so they are not holographic, and I must apologize about the low quality of the reproduction. Shall we begin?"

It was quite dark.

On the screen—

At first, the sea. It was from a boat's viewpoint, clearly; for the angle of the horizon dipped and straightened abruptly. The water sparkled; the sun was high. The unfamiliar two-dimensional quality made it seem like a painting that moved. And the colors were bright, unlike the real world. Surely the sea was not that blue . . .

Through the water a boat moved. It was far bigger than the two boats Ryoko had ridden in, and it rived the water easily. The camera followed this boat, sometimes going blurry with the spray.

In the distance, beyond the ship, a whale danced on the water! Ryoko's heart took a turn at this, for she had never seen whales in the sunlight, but only in gray places and in twilight. Its body rose all at once, flashing white light-flecks, the curve of its leap a song—and Ryoko knew what was going to happen next. Her stomach churned with the terror of it.

The boat changed direction and charged through the water, the camera zoomed close and Ryoko saw the name of the boat, the *Murasaki Maru,* and then they were on the deck and she saw the crewmen, some barechested, others in casual clothes, huddled on one side and pointing, excitedly . . . they were laughing, some of them, they were jeering! And behind them—

The whale leapt and dove, its tail suspended above the water for a too-long moment, defying gravity; then the fan of its tail vanished behind the curve of the boat. The camera zoomed over empty water, then another leap, then—

Zing! A spear in its flanks, blood rushing out, more blood than seemed possible from a single creature, and still the leap went on . . . and stopped short and fell back and thrashed against the frenzied water and then more sailors laughing laughing jeering jeering demons and the waves dancing—

Ryoko screamed. "Stop this! Stop this!" She tried to close her eyes but the pain shot through her eyelids, had to close her eyes even if she tore her eyelids and she tried and felt blood dripping over her eyes and still the whale thrashed and the men laughed and laughed—

And a voice came booming through the room: "This is what we are guilty of. We have killed our forefathers, we have killed them horribly, without shame, we have used their dead bodies to light our homes and to wash our bodies and to make perfumes and to fertilize our crops, these creatures whose dreams created the Japanese people . . ."

"Make it stop Didi make it stop" she screamed.

. . . *tired* . . . such a small voice, so pitiable! And the big voice went on, a droning accompaniment to the slaughter.

She was screaming without any end now screaming over and over and she heard Josh screaming too, and still the voice pounded at her and the whale died and the water crashed and the hatred shone through the eyes of the sailors and the whale died and the whale died and

Lights. Dizziness.

Quickly the black samurai released them.

Ryoko could not move. When she was free she merely closed her eyes, squeezed them to shut out the glare, and found tears streaming down her cheeks. *We did this to them!* her mind raged. *It's true, it's true, we deserve to die!*

A small voice in her mind: . . . *tired* . . .

"Shall we have lunch?" Kawaguchi said brightly.

Josh followed behind as they were led down narrow, whitewashed corridors to the next place. It was a dining room.

A high ceiling, *tatami* floors, a low table veneered in imitation onyx, four cushions arranged around the table, white silk embroidered with the character *shi*—death—in red, in the elegant, cursive style of calligraphy.

This was one character Josh had learnt to recognize in the days at Shikoku.

They removed their shoes; attendants moved *shoji* in place, so they were enclosed in a small space, and Kawaguchi said, "Come, eat."

They sat crosslegged on the *tatami* against the cushions, Josh very awkwardly. He was shaken from the movie. He saw that Ryoko was moving like an automaton, and that he had to help Didi gently to his seat. Kawaguchi watched their various struggles to be seated in a detached, offhand way. "With our population dwindling," he said, "nature is once more abundant, food is available aplenty . . ."

Josh gripped Didi's small body, which was trembling violently.

"What's the matter with that child?" Kawaguchi snapped. "Can't he talk for himself?"

"Leave him be," said Josh angrily. "You've no right to subject him to this, he's only an idiot kid—" The lie tasted sour, now that he knew what his brother really was. And he shot a glance at Ryoko, who was motionless, petrified. Were the two of them communicating? He felt shut out, alone. . . . "Leave him be!" he said again, with such hatred that Kawaguchi recoiled a little before putting on his mask of genial sarcasm again.

Four Deathbound women entered, their white robes brushing the floor, rustling softly. Each carried a lacquerware tray.

Josh closed his eyes and saw the harpoon rush to meet the leaping whale and the spurt of blood—"I can't eat!" he said. But the food was being set before them and he was hungry and the scent was tempting.

Blood, darkening the water through his nausea . . . "I'll be sick!"

"Ah," Kawaguchi said mildly. "The burden of guilt is coming to light at last. You are all beginning to see things as they really are. We'll save you yet. But now you must eat, you must be strong. You have some heavy decisions to make, although we at Shikoku have no doubt as to their outcome . . . when you decide, you will feel clean again."

Ryoko said, "If you are the ruler of Japan—and my father is dead and so, it is claimed, is Takahashi—how do you have time to be our jailer?" Josh saw how she was striving to control herself.

Kawaguchi's face darkened. And then he indicated the trays with his chopstick, and said, "Eat, eat, eat!"

Josh looked at his tray. There was a plate of raw fish, innocuous enough, of different types, arranged to resemble many-petaled imaginary flowers, white and red; a bowl of *miso* soup, rice and pickles. *Is he poisoning us?* came the thought. But he was ravenous suddenly. "Perhaps we *should* eat," he said to Ryoko, who was staring at emptiness. "We didn't come here to commit suicide by starvation, we can't let their rantings get to us, *please*—"

Slowly, Ryoko nodded.

"That's the spirit exactly, Yoshiro and Ryoko," said Kawaguchi, beaming at them.

"It's poisoned, isn't it?" said Josh suspiciously.

"Ha, why should we force your hands?" said Kawaguchi. "You have indeed a low opinion of our integrity. . . . but try this," he said, pointing with his chopstick to one of the kinds of *sashimi*. "This particular raw fish is a delicacy seldom found these days. Oh, of course, the *hotate-sashi*, the raw scallops you see there, are rare also . . . but this red fish here . . ."

Josh glanced at Ryoko. She smiled wanly, and the two of them picked up their chopsticks, carefully separated them, dipped the fish in the *shoyu* sauce, ate.

It was quite tasty. It was unlike the raw fish he had had before; it had a sweetness to it, a hint, almost, of red meat—

Abruptly, Kawaguchi stood up. "Enough!" he cried. "Shame on you! A delicacy of the old times, yes indeed . . . raw whaleflesh! You filthy cannibals!"

Josh saw Ryoko's face pale. A retching sensation crawled up his throat. He threw the plate onto the *tatami*, cracking it and sending fish-slices flying. All the images they had forced him to look at surged in his mind, the wounded whale whipping against the waves, the seamen mocking, the murder the murder the blood—he couldn't help himself and vomited onto the table.

Kawaguchi burst out in savage laughter. "No shame! No shame!" he grated. Through his revulsion Josh saw that Ryoko was weeping uncontrollably, pounding her fists against the false onyx tabletop—

"You tricked us!" he said. "Your brainwashing is worthless . . ." he spat out the words. "We'll never give in now, never, never—" But as he said this he knew that he had never wanted so much to die, to end this feeling of sickness, to find the wombwarmth of the water—and saw nothing but blood, gushing from the whale, gushing into the sunlight.

"Kill me! Kill me!" Ryoko was screaming, and a thin smile played on the lips of Kawaguchi. Josh put his arms around Ryoko and Didi and they huddled together, and the laughter of Kawaguchi became one with the laughter of the seamen, pitiless—

A sighing filled the air, like the surf clattering pebbles on the glass beach on Hawaii—

"Didi," he whispered, trying to break through the wall around his brother, "if you can hear me, help me help me . . ."

Bro—ther— A tiny voice. And the sighing, veiling the small voice, crescendoed still.

"Who's making that repulsive noise?" said Kawaguchi. The surfsound rose from whisper to shatter—

Josh drew comfort from the sound out of his past. He rose and faced Kawaguchi, defiant. "You can't win," he said softly.

Ryoko stood up now. "Kawaguchi," she said, "you are too weak to understand us. I know that you only work for Takahashi—"

Kawaguchi lifted his hands, as if warding off something evil.

"I know that Takahashi didn't die. This whole plan, this whole crazy dream of Ending and perfection . . . it could only come from a mind both great and sick, both poetic and diseased. You're a small man, Kawaguchi—my father even said so—caught between one man's dream and another man's nightmare . . ."

"Ai, I can't cope with this!" said Kawaguchi. "I've failed! Only Death Lord can make you see reason!"

"THAT WILL BE ENOUGH, KAWAGUCHI." A thunderous voice, rising from an unseen source.

"Takahashi!" Ryoko said, gripping Josh's hand.

"DO NOT CALL ME THAT! I AM DEATH LORD. YOU, KAWAGUCHI, HAVE PLAYED TOO MANY GAMES WITH MY CHILDREN. YOU MAY RETIRE TO THE CHERRY ORCHARD. BE THANKFUL THAT I DO NOT HAVE YOU THRUST, STILL LIVING, ONTO THE CONVEYOR BELT, TO BE DISPOSED OF LIKE A DISEASED CADAVER."

Josh said, "Who are you? Why do you need our deaths so badly?"

"You've eavesdropped on everything!" Ryoko shrieked. "You've spied on us, you've hidden microphones and speakers everywhere, playing with us . . ."

Kawaguchi had dropped to his knees and bowed solemnly. "I thank you for permission to end my life," he said in a strangled monotone. At once black samurai poured into the dining room, and *shoji* were ripped down, and Josh saw that they were in an enormous hall, opening out on both sides on to sculpted gardens. And at the far end, on a dais above a low table, sat a man in black. And instinctively he knew he was looking at the black center of all these happenings.

From the corner of his eye he saw Kawaguchi leave the room, unnoticed by the black samurai or by the man at the far end of the hall.

"MY CHILDREN," said the voice, deep and echo-rich, "I AM YOUR FATHER, DEATH LORD, THE GREAT DREAMER, THE PROPHET OF ENDING, THE POET OF THE LAST LINE OF THE HAIKU. KAWAGUCHI'S TECHNIQUES OF 'PERSUASION' WERE JUVENILE AT BEST, MY CHILDREN. BUT NOW YOUR FATHER WILL TELL YOU EVERYTHING . . . COME FORWARD, MY CHILDREN. . . ."

Josh took a step forward—

In a moment, guards held them fast.

Chapter 21

Didi's consciousness seemed to detach itself from the body, seemed to be looking over the chamber from a vague height. It floated free, it penetrated the other minds in the room like a spring wind through open *shoji*. He saw—

Himself first. Stunted, pitiful, with the eyes closed, lost to the world. He was walled off completely now, for he knew that the moment he had seen in the preek's mind, in the hotel room with the crazy lights, was close . . . and he was terrified. And more alone than any of the others. His white kimono was askew. He reached out as it were to touch his own forehead: colder than ice, as though he were drawing all the heat inside, into the furnace, to turn it into something else.

Next to him his brother stood. Uncertain, defiant. The mind was turbulent, incoherent; for its values had been overturned, over and over again. But there was one thought, still strong: *Don't give up!*

And Ryoko: afraid and resigned. In her mind, the image of her father, mingled now with images of Josh, whom she could not understand but whom she had begun to love. Didi saw the strength of that love, and thought: *Brother, I'm giving you into good hands, true hands. . . .* Emotion choked him for a moment, so that he could not perceive anything.

He felt the minds of the guards, too: they had released their captives and were waiting just outside, in the twin gardens that flanked the audience chamber. They were empty minds, little ones, weak ones; the thoughts felt like dragonflies, buzzing by and dying.

And, facing them from a distance that seemed forever (for Didi could perceive each straw blade of the *tatami* as a separate entity, each hair's breadth between the strawstrands) was Takahashi.

The dark heart of the false universe.

They call it dreaming, *the whales,* he thought. *What they mean is to see with utter clarity, beyond that limit which humans describe as* uncertainty. *They see the fabric of the universe, the very packets of mass-energy whose dance creates the illusion of reality, and are able to transform it. And if I reached out far enough—*

Once Aaaaaioookekaia had dreamed a great dream; and had created a people, a race, half in her own image . . . and Didi saw that Takahashi too dreamed a great dream, in his own way; that he too struggled, in his hopeless, perverted way, to be like Aaaaaioookekaia. But his heart was twisted.

If I could reach him—

His brain fought to reach his vocal cords. They encountered a wall of terror. He sent his sighing through the air, making the air-waves dance.

Takahashi studied his three guests, appraising them, not speaking. Not smiling, not frowning. At the low table at his feet lay two objects: a samurai sword (clean metal, and Didi's mind skimmed the honed edge, smarting) and a teabowl . . . the most beautiful object in the world. The two objects had been placed on the table with great care, the curve of the sword nestling and mothering the asymmetrical stoneware.

Finally, Takahashi spoke. This time there was no artificial amplification.

In the huge chamber it sounded unnaturally soft; Didi felt the other two strain to catch the words.

"Ah, children." It was a restrained, elegant voice, faintly menacing though . . . "Come closer. Come closer. Come, I won't do anything to you. See, I've turned off the amplifiers. I want you to see me as I am."

The three of them moved forward, hesitantly. Didi's body sagged; the weight.

"Sit at my feet," said Takahashi, "and gaze at this teabowl. That's all; no recriminations, no heartrending scenes of guilt."

Didi saw *fujisan,* moved.

"It *is* beautiful, isn't it?" said Death Lord, in a voice that did not ask their opinion. And Didi felt that even Josh had sensed its eerie beauty. "It is art, and I want to tell you about another kind of art, so listen then. A million years ago the whales spawned us and thrust us into the world of men. But we were people of two faces, endlessly caught between the turmoil of 'pure' humanity and the whales' love of death . . . when the humans had ended the world, in their filthy, degrading, messy way, a prophet came to us. The meaning of the whale's appearance is surely plain: it is a death symbol, a call to return to the motherwomb, the darkness, the ocean of death!"

Death Lord's voice became more passionate. "Listen, my children who seek to blight this final artwork! Listen, I tell you . . . if all the history of our people were but a single haiku, would this not be the last line of it? And should we sit back and let nature, and messy mankind, write the final line? Should not every cherry blossom fall to its appointed place, and every real person . . . I mean, every true Japanese . . . seek a perfect death?

"Mark what I'm saying! When we have all fallen like cherry blossoms, earth will cover us. Summer grasses will spring up, like skin over a wound. Cicadas will sing far into the night. We will vanish like the autumn wind. We will be a completed thought." Takahashi was animated now, his eyes lit up, his mind far away. "And you and I—don't you see, we will all be ink-flecks in the writing of the haiku. We will all be particles of clay in the teabowl, held together by a dream of surpassing beauty . . . for the sake of the dream, we must all die. Calmly, without fuss, without argument."

He's terrible he's lost thought Didi *I have to reach him, I have to reach them all before they fall into the trap—*

Josh said, "I don't know who you think you are. All I know is that you've tricked us at every turn. You're crazy! It isn't the dream of a sane person. You've tracked us down, hunted us, brought us here, all for the sake of a flaw in your private, impossible insanity—"

"How dare you!" said Takahashi. "I'm showing you the true way—"

"No!" said Ryoko. "He's right. "Your 'truth' is rotted through and through with lies! You seeded the suicide mania by pretending to kill yourself! You made it not a choice but a requirement!"

Takahashi rose, his eyes blazing. "It was necessary," he said roughly. "I made a necessary sacrifice, I was a necessary catalyst for what must be. You know that the ending should be like this—" he pointed to the teabowl —"and not—and not like a shapeless lump of clay."

Didi thought *If I spin a great mental net and catch them all in it and make them see themselves as they are, if I could only penetrate the walls around him, around all of them, meld them merge them but it would need all my strength it would use up everything everything but I saw it in the mind of the preek, cold and unchangeable—*

"You understand nothing!" Ryoko shouted. She had shaken off all her reticence, all her defenses. "It was *I*, not you, who spoke with the whale. It's love, not hate and fear, that motivates them."

"And I am motivated by love too," said Takahashi, in a voice full of hate. "Love for beauty. Love for truth. When Buddha was enlightened, did he immediately enter Nirvana? No, it was his compassion for humanity that made him stay on in the suffering world for forty more years, preaching the way. *I could not die!* I wanted to, I wanted to!"

"Are you comparing yourself with Buddha now?" And Didi saw that Ryoko pitied the man. "Do you claim that all *this* is the result of *satori?* You think you are a Buddha, don't you? Don't you understand that the mere act of *wanting* to become one is enough to negate any possibility?"

"Don't provoke me!" Takahashi was pale now.

She's hurt him now thought Didi *I have to help them before it's too late I have to force their minds together—*

"I don't know what either of you are talking about!" cried Josh. "I came here to find something better than cleaning latrines for the dying. I came because I love my brother and I wanted him out of the mess we were in. I don't understand any of this Buddhism shit, and I don't care to! But I know that you're a liar. I know that you're a madman who's somehow warped the minds of all these people in Japan, who's somehow perverted everything they believed in to fit some warped reality of your own. You want to be like the whales. And you never will be! And you're a coward. I bet you wouldn't kill yourself, even after every other Japanese in the whole world had killed himself! You'd cling to your miserable life, you'd sit and stare at your sword all day and meditate and try to screw up the courage and keep trying and keep trying—"

The typhoon's coming thought Didi *it's too late to stop thinking now brother I love you*—

With a terrible animal howl Takahashi clasped the samurai sword in both hands and strode down from the dais, aiming for Josh's neck—

Oh freeze Didi commanded *oh freeze freeze freeze freeze freeze*. This sword hung in midair, frozen in the moment before murder! The boy's body burst into fever-sweat, and his mind strained and strained

And spoke in the true speech!

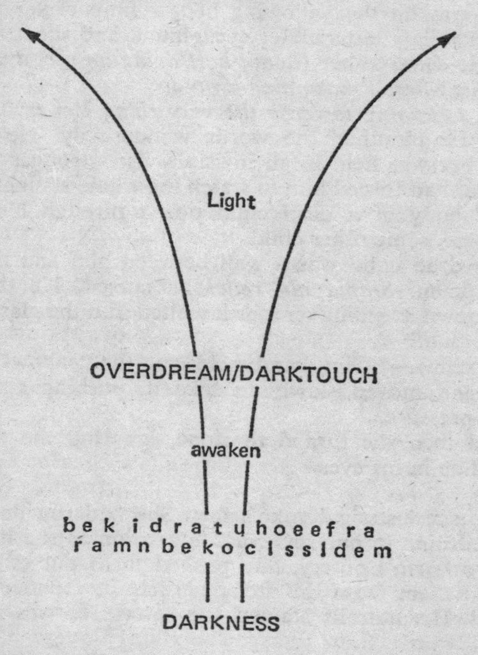

He seized their separate minds and isolated them, each in its own world. He watched each mind scurry through its private labyrinth. And he *dreamed* them. Loved them.

Josh was alone running barefoot on the glass beach.

It wasn't *the* glass beach because it had no end. His feet pounded the hard glass and it stole the heat from his body. The cold drove him on; he couldn't escape the cold because it was in himself.

There was no sky but a blue rippling, the force of the fusing sun filtering through water . . . it was an ocean floor. Josh ran without thinking, many miles, without a change in the landscape. Suddenly he thought: *I'm running in place.*

He stopped. He stood still. Above him a thunder-roar distilled by distance became the rush of blood inside his skull.

On the glass beach, *obasan* lay dying.

She was on the yellowing bed, a limp skeleton filmed over in yellow tatters. Her eyes, intent and silent, watched him. He came to her (*damn her! dying on me, dying . . .*)

Is this where I'm running away to?

Am I running towards the very thing I'm trying to escape? He mouthed the words wonderingly. He tried to move but was held in an invisible vise, stronger than the one that had forced him to watch the whale-slaughter.

The body of a dead child oozed through his fingers. *Didi*—no, some other child.

The dead child was a wall between him and the dying old woman. *Stupid old relic!* he cursed. He threw the child down, stepping on it as it melted into the glass.

"Obasan!"

"Yoshiro—" Her hand held out the teabowl to him. His hand moved slowly to take it, pushing against the water-pressure.

And then she turned to stone, ignoring the tears that welled up in his eyes.

The snow stung Ryoko's feet. She had run down from the bedroom in only her *yukata* as soon as she had heard the workmen's outcry. She pushed them out of the way, shooed them from the stone garden . . . under the tree he sat. His entrails stained the snow. He was not quite dead . . .

"Otosan!" she cried. "Please don't die, you can't leave me now I need you I love you—"

Ishida's face dissolved into the face of Takahashi!

Ryoko's hands shot back from the face. "You're making fun of me!"

The voice of Takahashi came from all corners of the

garden. "My child, my poor child; your father and I are one and the same, you know. Until you accept that—"

The snow-flurries pecked at her face like swarms of insects. Night was falling like a butcher's knife, the stars were glittercold; they were needles of bright light lancing into her. . . . *Father, why did you leave me? Don't you care? Why are you sending me away on this ship, first into the sea, now into the endless night?*

She battered the corpse with her fists, until her hands were raw-red with his blood and her own.

Creak . . . creak. . . .

There was a *give* in the old wood of the stairs as Takahashi trod them, as they spiraled to the top of the golden pagoda. When he reached the balcony he saw that he was quite alone, and that he faced the mirror-still lake and the low hills, and stood higher than the tops of the cherry trees. Takahashi ran to the diving board that edged out over the cement . . . his feet thudded. His robe flapped, heavy against his chest.

On the board stood Ishida. He faced Takahashi, serene, smiling. His garments were pure white, his face death-white, his hair snow-white. Takahashi bit his lip, angry. He had been cheated of his death scene!

"No," said Takahashi. "Step aside, it's for me to take the plunge, not you!"

"Ha!" It was the voice of that stupid, inelegant man Nakamura, Yoshiro Nakamura, Ryoko's new companion. "You don't dare, you don't dare, you coward, you coward—" Ishida's mouth had not opened.

"You were always the glib, skin-deep one!" Takahashi spun around to see the Abbot of the golden pagoda, his smile matching Ishida's.

"Don't mock me!" Takahashi pleaded . . . "Don't scold me, Abbot, I really want to do this act, I really want this beautiful thing so much, so much—"

"Then fight me for it!" Ishida's voice.

They were hypocrites, with their show of goodness and serenity! Takahashi sprang onto the diving board. The sunlight streamed on to his face, he drew his sword and lunged, straight for the side of the neck—

Thin air. Mocking laughter. "Ai!" He shouted, twisting around and thrusting, hard, into—

Emptiness.

"Phantoms! Mocking phantoms!" he gasped.

Ishida appeared, facing him from the edge of the board and smiling gently. Takahashi looked down and the distant ground seemed to jump up at him; the cherry trees swayed in the spring wind, showering the green with pink.

And he sprinted for the edge and the board wasn't under his feet and he saw teabowls revolving around his head and cherry trees flying fear fear and

"I'll never reach the bottom!" he said wonderingly, and the trees waltzed, and Ishida was in the trees and laughing and the Abbot standing there admonishing, *skin-deep, skin-deep,* and finally he knew he could reach the bottom whenever he chose to, he could crack like a teabowl on the ground but he couldn't choose he couldn't he couldn't—

Didi sat in that moment watching them in their mazes, piercing their minds.

"I have to cure them . . ."

His brain cells were burning, his body was burning, he had not been built to dream, not like the whales. His brain cells were shorting out but he knew he had to go on. He stretched himself tauter, trying to do the thing that he knew would kill him.

And he shouted out another word in the true speech of the whales, words that for humans can only be suggested as clumsy pictographs, a word of melding, trying to break them free of their cages—

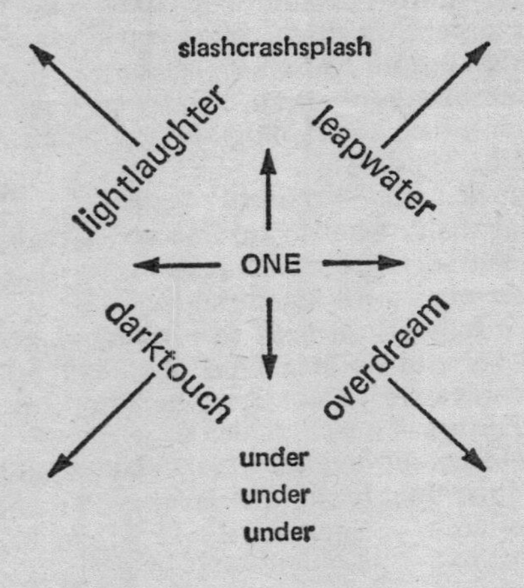

And the walls crumbled!

Ryoko awoke. Was it the hospital, where she opened her eyes to drabness and graying walls, or was it the prison of Shikoku, the darkness with the whispering voices? Both pictures blurred in front of her, and then—

Soft, red, glowing. A deep pulsing, like the inside of a giant living creature.

"Josh!" her own voice answered her, re-echoing to nothing. There were walls, living walls. But no fetid stench; instead, a sweetness, like incense in a shrine . . . and the deep pulsing vibrated like drums from the heart of a Shinto temple. It was warm here.

. . . and then Josh.

"I don't see any of this, I don't understand any of it," he said. "One minute I was flinching from the sword, now I'm . . . nowhere!"

"I don't know either . . . your brother has done this. Maybe he has found out how to save us."

"But will we be trapped here forever?"

"I don't know!" said Ryoko. "But I think that the sword is still coming at you, and that Didi has somehow gained us a reprieve, seized our minds. What did you see?"

"My grandmother." Josh shuddered. "I felt like crying. I didn't know that I cared about her that much. She never understood me! She was always trying to turn me into a model Japanese kid, she didn't see how outdated and irrelevant and stupid that was. But I miss her, now."

"I saw my father," said Ryoko slowly. "I always felt terrible that I didn't find him in the garden, dead, that I was told, that I became dead inside and couldn't cry enough."

"What's Didi doing? He's sending us ghosts to haunt us . . ."

"I don't think so. I think he's trying to cure us, to make us whole again . . . we've had strange, unhealthy lives, you and I. You were always running from what they said you were, I was always in love with death, until I could see the Ishida Expedition as a kind of death, too: then I embraced it, I embraced the stars . . . but with such an aching emptiness inside me!"

They came together across the wet, phosphorescent floor. Shafts of red light broke the darkness, touching their faces, their clothes . . . between the leviathan heartbeats, they kissed.

And kissed again.

When they broke free, Ryoko said: "Once before I had the feeling of being in this place. It was when the whale took over my mind, to talk to my father and the others. I could touch the minds of all of them, and I was in a warm place, like the heart of a Buddha . . . yes, I recognize it now."

"It's all right, Ryoko." He touched her with hungry hands.

"Do we dare?" she whispered. "Are we profaning this place?"

"No! No!" said Josh urgently. "This is our place, my brother made it for us!"

Fluid as a painter's brushstrokes, the yellow-tall grass rippled in the summer wind. When the wind ceased, the haze began, hurting Hideo's eyes. A dragonfly flew past. He snatched at it with his little fingers—

"Follow, child!" He turned to see his teacher. But it wasn't his teacher; it was the immortal poet Basho, the greatest master of haiku, dressed in *kabuki*-like sixteenth-century dress, his hair slicked back. Hideo Takahashi rubbed his eyes. *Ai, a boy like me should be out snuffing out dragonflies, and not have to listen to lectures from stuffy poets out of the past.*

"Shall I beat you, scoundrel?" came the poet's voice, without any malice. Takahashi knew it was all in fun. But he chose that moment to scamper up to the poet; and he looked up at him and saw the haunted eyes, and knew himself for what he was: a child playing at being a man, a child with grand visions built of straw.

The master laughed and said: "My, what a solemn look you have, Takahashi. Why don't you compose a haiku for me?"

Hideo felt trapped. "Master—" he said. "You are the greatest composer of haiku of all time! How should I compete. . . ?"

"Who asked you to compete, youngling?" The master was stern. His features creased earnestly, like old paper. "Why do you always see everything in terms of competing? Have you no sense of self-worth at all, that you must always be measuring your efforts *objectively,* as if that were really possible? The haiku!" he commanded.

Stiffly, Takahashi bowed. His mind grabbed the first thing he could think of.

The dragonfly. How he wanted to squeeze it to death between his fingers! To be in command of it . . . it fluttered past him again, a red buzzing tapering into air. "Ah yes," he said. "Here it is—

Red dragonfly
Now pluck its wings from it!
. . . a pepperpod."

He beamed suddenly, expecting praise.

"Well done, my son," said the great poet, sounding very disturbed.

"What do you mean, master?"

"You have pointed up very distinctly the difference between a random collection of seventeen syllables and a haiku! Your rubbish negates the very idea of a haiku. Now, to convert it into true poetry, it must go like this" —he closed his eyes and there seemed to be a sudden stillness:

"Red pepperpod
Now give it wings!
. . . a dragonfly."

Hideo opened his mouth in dismay. Then, appallingly, he burst into tears . . . the face of Basho flickered oddly, reminding him of someone else—

You were always the glib, skin-deep one!

Hideo Takahashi bawled like a baby.

The whale-love that burned its way through Didi's brain was as far beyond human love as human love is beyond the mating instincts of worms or paramecia. It was compassion beyond life. It was a hard thing, terrible, incandescent as a star's heart.

Now he drew forth strands from the three minds and wove them into ever-intertwining matrices. And loved the three of them, even the dark one, with a joy that was like pain.

(He longed for the ocean now. For he was trapped between the two worlds. The ocean and death were one; for all he could give the ones he loved was life itself, his own life.)

And felt the life gushing from him now. But he had to hold on a little longer . . . they had to be ready to leave the inner world he had led them to. If he lost his grip now, if he died now, they would be lost within *for ever.*

"If only I were not so weak, if I were only a true whale . . ."

From cell to cell of gray matter the burning raced, like a chain reaction, like the very bombs that had destroyed the world.

Her face is *beautiful,* Josh decided. Everything about it seemed new to him. It was a plain face though; the beauty was gathered up inside her, only to be seen with the right eyes . . . the two of them rose from the moist floor of the cavern. The slow, heartbeat drumming never stopped. Josh saw that the walls, as far as he could see, up to the cathedral-like roof, were aglow with stars. Phosphorescence, that is; like the sea some nights. They clung to each other, reluctant to separate. But then Ryoko darted to the wall and ran her hands along the warm surface, and the sparks made lightflecks on her fingers. He went to her.

"It's so beautiful here!" she said. "I could wander around forever. It's warm, it's like a home, a childhood room."

Josh tried to remember his own childhood, before he was ten, on Hawaii. Had he had a room of his own, was there a warmth there? No memories came. "Ryoko, we have to leave, eventually," he said. But he could imagine no way.

In the distance, a baby cried.

"What was that?" said Ryoko.

"A child, lost here somehow . . . let's go and find it." He thought of Didi for a moment, and felt a strange burning sensation in his mind. But the feeling drifted away. "Come on," he said, "let's figure out where it's coming from."

They touched hands lightly and set off in the general direction. A darkness crept over them, and before they knew it they could see nothing. But the crying grew louder, more anguished.

"What an awful thing to do," said Ryoko, "to leave a baby here . . . Come on, it must be coming from right in front of us. I can't see!"

The lights in the walls were dead. The darkness was thick, like a dungeon. Josh felt Ryoko's fingers curling around his own, and they were his only link to sanity. The bawling grew louder. It wasn't a baby's bawling; more like an older child who was so desperate he had regressed to babyhood.

"Let me out! Let me out!"

They could make out the words in between the hysterical sobbing now.

"How can we help it?" said Ryoko.

"I don't know. Nothing is logical in this place . . . perhaps if we call to him, if we give him a part of ourselves . . ."

(It's Didi, it must be . . . he thought, I have to get through to him!)

"We must have compassion," said Ryoko.

They held hands and listened to the desperate crying; they were powerless to stop it, but they projected at the strange voice all the love they had learned to give—

A slit of light in the darkness parted, and a boy stepped out, arms outstretched . . . "Thank you for loving me," he said. It was Didi's voice. "Thank you for freeing me!" And the child ran to embrace them both, and Josh shouted "Didi, you can talk now, you've finally conquered your terror!" and he hugged the boy, a slim nothing in his arms, but the body grew and grew and became

Takahashi.

"I've been tricked!" Josh cried, and dropped the child like a burning object.

He hated Takahashi. He knew this. He had known it before he had met the man, this despicable murderer. The hate in him should well up now, he should strangle the man with his own hands. . . .

I hate you!

But the words did not come out.

The hate had been flushed out of him.

"No," he said, "I don't hate you now. I understand you."

"You are part of us two," Ryoko said.

Takahashi was changed, Josh thought. Either the scales had fallen from his own eyes, and he now saw the truth inside the artifice . . . or the man had dropped the artifice and shown the unhappy child beneath it. "I don't hate you at all. In fact, I . . . love you," he said.

The three of them joined hands, Takahashi in the middle.

And then the world shook and roared! "It's an earthquake, quick, find a doorway," Josh said. Was this Ueno

Park, then, the day he had met Ryoko for the second time?

Light sundered the darkness. The roof began to split slowly down the middle, revealing a blinding white light. The earthquake started again. A tremor threw them up, and they were flying upwards, into the shattering whiteness—

Into a starlight night over an ocean—

A whale leapt and shattered into pieces before he hit the waves. The three of them soared above the dark water, above the island where silver needles pointed at the sky, and

Fragments of the moon flew together with a crash, and there was one moon again, and the stars and

Got to bring them out now got to bring them out Didi gasped weakly now with his final ounce of strength awake awake awake awake awake

The sword shattered, shards scattered on the *tatami.*

Takahashi was weeping. Without any shame. "I'm a coward! Coward! I could never have killed myself at the end of it! I don't deserve to live, please kill me, kill me!"

Josh and Ryoko went to him. Together they lifted him up.

"Hideo," Ryoko said, gently, as to a child who has done wrong without knowing it: "There is no haiku without the lines on the page, without the memory of the words. Your dream was a beautiful thing, Hideo. Remember that always. It was *too* beautiful, even. But there must be survival, or there will have been no dream . . ."

Summer sounds stole in on their senses: chirping of crickets from the gardens, croaking of frogs.

"We were gone only a few minutes, Ryoko," said Josh. "I wonder how he did it . . ."

"I don't wonder," said Ryoko.

"I've failed!" Takahashi wept. "There's nothing left for me, the dream is broken, I've seen myself for what I am, a dreamer of distorted truth, a liar . . ."

Josh said, "Takahashi, we saw you as you are too. When we went through that experience . . . pieces of our past, like jigsaw pieces, were rearranged and . . . we *saw* each other! The way people never see each other, down to the core! And we don't despise you anymore."

"Hideo," said Ryoko, "you can come with us to Aishima."

"Yes!" said Josh, excited. "You have the right, as much as we do!"

Takahashi's sobbing subsided a little. "That can't be," he said, "I've stood for the destruction of Aishima for so long. I'm your enemy. You should kill me and forget."

"No!" said Ryoko. "The meaning of Aishima is this: that there is no longer any guilt. It does not matter to the stars. We leave our homes behind us, and perhaps also our hate, our honor, our disgraces . . . we begin a new haiku."

For the first time there came a light in Takahashi's eyes. "A chance to dream again."

"A healed dream," Josh added.

"Yes," said Takahashi.

And then they noticed Didi. He was quite stiff, like a statue, and his face was utterly still, his eyes serene and clear as though he were gazing on nirvana.

"Once before, when I was a young man . . . in the face of an old man who killed himself . . . I saw this same serenity," said Takahashi. "From that moment to this I burned with jealousy of it. But no longer."

He clapped his hands, a startling noise in the silence, for the guards to come and dispose of the child's body. And then they three went out, through the open *shoji,* into the summer garden.

Only the teabowl remained.

Part Four

THE LAST LINE OF THE HAIKU

Ara umi ya
Sado ni yokotau
ama no gawa

(Tempest on the sea!
And, flung out over the Island of Sado—
A star river . . .)

—Basho (1644–1694)

Chapter 22

AUTUMN, 2024

Light speared the leaping whale.

For a long time he had floated on the edge of dream. But now the slapcrash of his body segued again and again into the whisperrhythm of the waves, and again and again he broke the surface, sending sprayswirls into the light-dappled water. . . .

He was an old whale. His mind had turned so inward on itself that he perceived directly the unity of all matter and energy. His thoughts touched, lightly, the distant stars . . . for he had loosed the earthbonds, had banished desire, had become pure music. There was nothing left but joy.

So he was drawn towards extinction, as towards a lover, as towards the end-beginning womb-death perfection, death oh death. Into the deepness he dove, and then he broke water again, soaring, singing, floating, flying. The deathdance was in him now.

And now he sensed others dancing alone. Bubbles of aloneness in the raging sea. But dissolving, slowly dissolving into oneness. Into the great dream.

The dream!

For an Ending of all Endings, there must be a great

dream, the greatest dream that ever was, a dream more magnificent than the dream of Aaaaaioookekai, even. . . .

He sang, his slow song harmonizing with the songs in the distance, but effortlessly, the music falling into place as though preordained. They were songs of Ending all, snatches of awesome beauty tossed to the endless music of the waves.

A slow yearning awoke in him—

To the source of the deathdance!

For days he swam, led by the others' singing, until he reached the place where the water shouted its final joy.

Takahashi paced the corridors.

Paced the garden.

Ripped open the door that led to the room—

. . . Wind through shattered *shoji,* chilling . . . leaves cascading slowly on the unkempt *tatami* . . . a low table with a shattered sword and an abandoned teabowl . . .

Takahashi pulled the *shoji* too abruptly. It made no difference. The wind whistled as ever. He shrugged. Through the torn paper he could see the garden outside the tea room: overgrown, the grass age-yellowed, the stones of the rock garden scattered, stutter-riddling the harmony. . . .

Suddenly he could no longer remain in the room. He drew the *shoji* open, letting in the wind, and then he stepped out into the garden, his feet finding the path under the tangle; and he walked to the gate, hanging half-hinged from the occidental-style brick wall. Autumn was cold this year.

"Death Lord—" A breathless voice.

He saw Kawaguchi standing by the gate. "So you never killed yourself," he said. But he smiled as he said it. "I am no longer Death Lord." He referred to himself with the I-pronoun for ordinary persons, not the one reserved for emperors.

"You rescinded the orders . . ."

"Of course, of course." They stepped out of the garden onto the slope that overlooked the lake. Far away, the false Mount Fuji rose over the water. There was the cliff where thousands had leapt to their deaths. There in the distance was the amusement park, that cunning, deadly conceit. "Where are Ryoko and Josh?"

They were coming up the slope now, he saw. Arm in arm. They were beautiful. Kawaguchi pointed to them.

"Good," Takahashi said. "For I want them both to see this new thing."

"Yes."

"And you . . . you will not journey on the starship?"

Kawaguchi lowered his head.

"You're a coward, Kawaguchi."

"Yes."

The two lovers were beside them now. Takahashi could not meet their eyes at first. He had closeted himself in his hidden rooms for some weeks now, trying to understand what had happened. At first he had brooded over Ishida—from the very first days of their rivalry, Ishida had always won. And he had won again, no matter how hard Takahashi had tried to cheat. But the dead were meaningless. You couldn't contemplate them forever. He thought he was ready to go to Aishima now.

His eyes darted briefly from Josh to Ryoko. They seemed blank, fresh, like pages on which haiku had yet to be composed. He looked away very quickly. He did not want to remember the terrible fire they had been through together. He did not want to be open to such searing intimacy again.

The two waited; the silence made him nervous, so he spoke. He said, "Look. Over there. Ahead of you. I have just given the order." And he pointed to the spurious Fuji—

Their eyes followed the arrow of his arm, and then he saw it too—

The mountain dissolving into the gray air. Like a lap-dissolve in an ancient movie, making the world a celluloid thing, not real.

"Rejoice, Ishida!" he shouted impulsively, his voice sounding feeble against the wind.

"My father doesn't rejoice," Ryoko said quietly. Josh said nothing, although some inarticulate emotion seemed on the brink of surfacing.

Takahashi thought for a moment of two winds—the wind around them and the sea-wind made by a cupping of hands over ears or by covering them with an old teabowl. The sound of the rushing blood. *I carry the wind inside me,* he thought. Somehow his spirit was lifted by the thought.

Then they saw, in the aftershimmer of the holographic Mount Fuji, the ruins that had lain hidden since the creation of the death land. It was a crumbling oil refinery. . . .

A forest of broken funnels, end-broken, impotent, tried to soar from the rubble. Husks of buildings stood, earth-colored, veined with creeping plants. No master of ikebana could have made a flower arrangement so exquisite, so tastefully sensual. The gray of the sky, the mottled almost-red almost-green surfaces, the crumbling, spent towers.

"Reality," he said, "is not a work of art. There is no perfect Ending—only perfect moments that seem to be eternities, moments made sublime by their very transience."

Even as he said it it rang false, though he knew it was true. Although he had learnt much about truth, he had lost his power to put truths into words, to make words into ringing crystallizations of great thoughts. He saw that the young couple were ignoring him now, interested only in themselves. Perhaps they too felt uncomfortable, did not need to be reminded of that terrible intimacy, of the merging.

He watched the ruin of the refinery for a long time. He found himself weeping without knowing why. "This isn't a sad moment," he protested, half to himself.

"Perhaps—" Kawaguchi ventured, and he was like a buzzing fly in summer that one is too amiable to slap, "perhaps they are tears of joy, Takahashi."

Without another word Takahashi turned back towards the house.

—To the source of the deathdance—

He felt them, then, with shouts of joy that shook the water and made a music like the old tides had made once when the moon still wrought its magic on the waves, and when he reached the place he was already giddy with the light, half-blinded by it, drunk with it—

The light!

The water tasted foul now, but he had forgotten the old sweetness. Now the plankton were strange, tainted by a conflict far-off in space or time, he could not tell which; but he did not remember how he had once gorged on the taste-rich water. And now all the other things were fading from his memory too—his sense of self, his own rebelliousness—was it not he who had sought out the girl, the earthchild, so long ago? or had it been some other one?

The light made the past and the future dark. His brain sang utter serenity.

The light! The light! This was the place then—

There! They clove the water, a hundred whales or more, loving death together, sharing the light, pouring the last vestiges of their identities into the light, becoming one with the light—

Criss-crossing, arcs crashed and lashed the sea into tempest! The whale danced with the others, throwing his life into the light. They leapt up high in unison, in echo, in counterpoint, twining the twitterings of their songs with the pedalpoint knell of the word of melding:

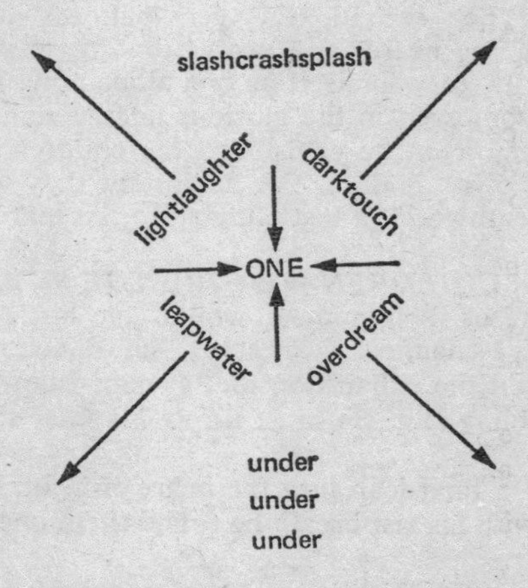

and then particles streamed collided flickered annihilated in infinitesimal notches of time that were eternities, in that region of reality that human scientists had once named *uncertainty*, and the whale perceived them, and they danced the dance with the virtual photons and the supergiants and the white holes gushing, and they touched the edges of the far stars—

A GREAT DREAM! WE WILL MAKE A FINAL GREAT DREAM, A FINAL GENE-CHANGE TO CELEBRATE THE ENDING!

—and gazed in a fevertrance at the light and found light behind the light and light exploding behind the light exploding behind the light exploding behind the light exploding behind the—

WE GIVE UP THE WATER'S WARMTH. WE GIVE UP OUR LONG LIVES. TO OUR CHILDREN WE GIVE ONLY OUR DREAMS. ONLY THE JOY.

—and overdream behind the light and laughter across the light—

WE RELINQUISH OUR INTELLIGENCE. WE RELINQUISH THE GREAT BODIES THAT HAVE HOUSED THE GREAT BRAINS WITH THE POWER TO MOTHER THE DREAMS. THERE WILL BE NO MORE DREAMINGS AFTER THIS GREAT DREAM.

—over the sealeapstarstrewnsilverpointedislandhighhigh-laugh! laughhighhighislandpointedsilverstrewnstarleapsea over the—

Millions per second, the gene-patterns danced and shifted, coming nearer and nearer the dream-pattern. The whale hardly knew himself as one alone now. Leaping, he was still submerged in the glorious light, living the dream. But for a moment he envisioned the children of this last dream, his own children. For an instant they would frolic over the deathworld, a last clinging to the material, before they . . .

TO OUR CHILDREN WE GIVE THE SKY!

Soon one of their number would give birth to the new children, sea-changed, evanescing, sun-dancing . . . now he must fight the exhaustion that swooped down over him like a tumbling sky. He must throw his final strength into the dream.

He took a final leap into the heart of light, he fell into darkness, with his last breath he found them one.

Days later, black bloated corpses speckled the water like lumps of onyx set in gold, the sunlight glancing off the sea. The deathdance was over. . . .

But one like Aaaaaioookekaia had spawned the children of the great dream.

The children of the dream gathered, like distant mists, and drifted towards Aishima, the island where silver needles pointed up from the wild sea, up to the star river.

In the dream they were all standing at the gate to the inner courtyard of the ruined temple. Ryoko saw how the wild grasses had run wild everywhere, filling the crannies of the timbers, thrusting through the stone lanterns, pushing through the cracks in the broken tiles. There was no feel of death here, she thought as she entered the graveyard. It was high summer in the dream; the sun touched everything, and the grass itself was warm and living to the touch.

Ishida's grave was almost buried under the summer grass. Only the plain wooden marker, with its painted inscription in the cursive, broke through the sea of green like a buoy in the waves. The wind in the grass was hot.

Ryoko did not know what to do or say now that she had reached her father's grave. She understood that it was a dream, that she would never in fact fulfill her initial objective in leaving Aishima for Tokyo. Around her the Temple swam a little in the haze. . . .

I'm sorry, Father, she was thinking, *for not believing you. For trying to die, so long ago.* Now what was she going to say? *My love for you is stronger than my love for myself. Compassion is stronger than honor. And love is stronger than death.*

These were the three lessons she had learnt when she passed through the melding of minds in the Death Land into a moment of more than human awareness.

And now there was one thing she must do before the journey—

She must turn her back on the grave and walk out through the gateway, leaving behind all her pain as an offering to the dead—

In her sleep she cried out and felt Josh's arms around her. Suddenly she was awake. Silence was heavy around them. They were in a western-style bed in a room overlooking the lake. The unfamiliar softness was making her uneasy. . . .

A sudden anguish lanced her, faded—

A shrill cry broke the stillness. A seagull? How could it be? They were so far from the ocean.

Josh whispered, "You're hurting still. You still want to visit your father's grave, to finish your own poem. . . ."

"How did you know?" she said, turning away from him.

The gull's cry, bringing to mind—

. . . the cry of the gull as they huddled in the rickety boat in Yokohama harbor, the gull-cry that broke through the babble of the banquet on the day that Takahashi had pretended to kill himself, a millennium ago it seemed. . . .

The memories were fading now. They were dissolving as the false Mount Fuji had dissolved. She searched for the ache she had felt only moments before, but found nothing. "We've got to go to Aishima now," she said.

"Tomorrow."

Father! Aaaaioookekaia! The Sound of water!

She clasped him to her close, guiding him into her with her hand. Now she was the sea, and he the leaping whale.

Chapter 23

WINTER, 2024/2025

. . . a hospital smell in the air. . . .

Ryoko struggled to wake up. She didn't know where she was. She remembered another hospital in the unreachable past, a gray-walled hospital in Tokyo where she'd lain and thought over and over, *I'm sterile I'm sterile—*

"Where. . . ?"

"Aishima." Doctor Doane's face swam in front of her, resolved. "It's a success, Ryoko, we did it."

"Yes." She was so tired! A deathsleep was calling from deep within her . . . she forced her eyes open. The room was gray as the other one had been, before. One window faced the sea, and the wind sang salt-tanged songs to her. She was remembering . . . they'd broken the stasis shield on one of the whale ova according to the instructions Ryoko had received from the whale that day in Yokohama. The experts had pronounced it quite human, apparently. Then why had the whale taken the trouble to say, "These are my children"? But then the Japanese people, too, had been his children. Ryoko understood. When the news was brought to her she'd said, "It stands to reason. Suppose we came to a planet without oceans, or with seas frozen solid? The whale thought of that. The gene-changes in the eggs . . . are hidden ones, like those that first created the Japanese people. We will seem the same, we will grow together, we will merge, perhaps. . . ."

Then, when she had said, "I want you to implant the ovum you unshielded in my womb," Doctor Doane had smiled at her. Now he smiled again.

"A child of yours will walk among the stars," he said, switching to English as soon as she seemed wide awake. They had gotten into the habit of using English on Aishima; Ryoko, Josh and Takahashi were the only ones who spoke Japanese reasonably well, and the caucasian immigrants had lost all desire to learn it. Ryoko smiled back at him.

"And you won't go?"

"I'm a coward."

"No, Nathan, you're not," Ryoko said. She propped herself up in the bed. "You stood by my father . . ."

Nathan Doane said, "There was something I wanted to learn." He looked away, out of the window. "When I was a student in the old country, in New England, they were on the verge of a breakthrough in physics, you know. They'd seen strange violations of the natural laws within the limits of the uncertainty principle, they'd even started to theorize that subatomic particles might have consciousness, outlandish ideas like that, all v ·y mystical . . . I wanted to find something concrete to understand, something complex and graspable, like a crystal or a musical score. But your whales have shown me what I lacked, because they have dreams that fashion reality. Now I understand how reality is the confluence of countless dreams. The journey that I have to take now is not up there, it's in here." He tapped his forehead, laughing lightly, walked briskly from the room.

"Wait—" Ryoko didn't finish her thought.

She thought instead of the child she would have and of where they were going:

Tau Ceti.

In the sign of The Whale.

Josh left Takahashi and the *go* board and walked towards the hut he shared with Ryoko. She was back from the hospital hut now, and she would be waiting for him. It was difficult, sometimes, to deal with the new, affable, warm Takahashi; he had been simpler when he was a figure of evil. Josh would never be quite at ease with him; he would never accept him as Ryoko seemed to.

It was night, and in the morning the first of the rockets would leave. He saw their silhouettes now, a forest of black obelisks against the fire-point-speckled star river. They had been unremarkable days, these last days.

What do I know, he thought, about *"Endings in beauty" and all their fancy philosophy? It's not death I care about! It's the future.* All the awesome events that had killed his brother and given him new people to love now left him with one burning desire—

The stars! I want them, I want them!

And now he saw the stars and he knew this desire that was like pain. He knew it for a primal human longing, not a longing of the whales. And he knew himself to be a human, not a man with a whale's mind. The desire had grown in him ever since they'd driven away from the Death Land in Takahashi's car—no chauffeur now, just Takahashi himself driving—in the summer sunlight.

He saw the stars and wondered if the starship that the Russians had abandoned so long ago was among them. He didn't think of the journey. He didn't think that he himself would not live to see an alien sunlight. He saw only the end of the journey, only the glittering destiny, because after all he was a human, and humans are quick to shrug off suffering when they see the distant light.

He stumbled for a second, then braced himself against the cold and hurried towards the hut.

They were to leave in shifts, and this first takeoff was not Ryoko's; she was due to go up in a day or two. All of them had gone to the other side of the island to see the rocket launched. But Ryoko had come down to the beach by herself, seeking a moment of solitude. It would be hot and glaring even on this side of Aishima, the side that faced Japan. It was a brilliant day now, but cold. In the fine black volcanic dust that was the island's beach, tiny sparkles threw back the sunlight.

She watched the sea. It was quite calm; in the old days, when there had been tides, the sea would never have been this calm here.

She tried to see Japan, tried to imagine her field of perception widening to encompass the distant shore. And she thought of the whale, missing him. She wished she could talk to him again. There had been no sight so heartbreaking, so beautiful, as the first time the whale had broken water and the waves had spoken to her. . . .

She tried to remember. But memories were fading. Even the face of the child Didi . . . the memory surfaced for a second, then dissolved.

Then an uneasiness fell on her from out of the clear blue sky.

She looked across the sea to the other horizon . . . was that a cloud, a smudge in the infinite blueness? Ryoko tensed. The unease came again, a sharp, knife-twisty little thing inside her. *And she had felt it before.*

The smudge grew, whiting out an eighth of the sky. And then she understood the pain—

The deathdance! It must be happening out there somewhere, perhaps just beyond the limits of her vision, perhaps on the other side of the ocean. . . .

But Ryoko did not know yet of the great dream.

The cloud grew still more, creeping towards the island. She shivered. Fear leadened her heart.

She could make out tiny white flecks in the cloud now, and feel the deathdance in her bones, and she saw the specks that were dust-motes, swirling in the cloud, like stars in a distant galaxy, and then the cloud moved past her head and threw a sudden grayness over the sea and the sand-sparklets fizzled and died out—

Behind her, a slow rumble. The launch was about to begin, she thought in the back of her mind. Somewhere the countdown was sounding.

The cloud of white dots was blowing over the island now, circling the island, and over the rumbling she could hear cries like the highest notes of a shakuhachi flute, and then she saw that the white dots were seagulls—

And even as she saw that they were seagulls she knew that they were not seagulls but shape-mimics only, that they were the source of the tension in the air, the sense of impending death—

Without warning the roar took her! Nothing could be so loud! Her very bones quaked, a trembling took her and shook her and gripped her body and it was an avalanche a volcano a thunder a falling mountain overpowering the cries of the birds, and then she saw—

The birds had formed a rocket shape themselves and were aimed like an arrow towards a single point, hovering, waiting—

And she whipped around and had to squeeze her eyes

tight shut at once, and then the light battered her eyeballs and there was light behind the light, like water behind a dam, light behind the light and more light and she was forced to turn her head away and crush her fists against her eyes and bury her ears and still the sound burst over her—

And in that moment, in that tiny second before the unbearable light had forced her eyes closed, she had seen—

—a million gulls, dashing themselves against the flames! Dashing and sizzling and plummeting in mid-flight, and still coming in from out of the sky, rushing openwinged towards death!

And then she understood.

The whales had dreamed a final great dream. They had fashioned a moment to bridge the real and the dream. . . .

Just as the Japanese had sprung from a dream, so these birds. The last children of the whales. In making this last gene-change, they had relinquished their intelligence, they had relinquished everything except their love for death. And she had touched the edge of this dream, this great vision that concerned no man.

Not men, not Takahashi, not even my father, but they *have written the last line of the haiku. And yet through me, through my chancing to see what I have seen, a remembrance of this haiku will touch the distant stars.*

And Ryoko waited for the end of the roaring, a time that seemed forever.

It is said that just before dying, the immortal Basho composed the following haiku:

tabi ni yamite
yume wa kare no wo
kake meguru

(On the sick journey—
across the withered fields—
the dream runs still!)

Tokyo, Paris, Alexandria, Bangkok, Arlington: 1977–1980